BOOK ONE IN THE SPRINGVILLE TRILOGY

THE SON OF A PASTOR

AMBER RODRIGUEZ

Cover Design: www.canva.com

Paperback ISBN: 9798989923229

eBook ISBN: 97989923236

Website: www.amrbooks.com

Contents

Dedication Page

To all the brats who can't stand being told what to do but love to say make me, this one's for you.

TSOAP PLAYLIST

Unholy – Sam Smith (feat. Kim Petras)
Smoke + Mirrors – Leo Waters
Too Sweet – Hozier
Whatever She Wants – Bryson Tiller
Special Delivery – Chris Brown
Trouble – Camylio
Dangerous Hands – Austin Giorgio
Dreams, Fairytales, Fantasies - A$AP Ferg
(Brent Faiyaz & Salaam Remi)

Author's Note

Hey Bookish Babes and Bookworms! This book is a dark erotica romance novel and is a part of an interconnected trilogy, some of the plots carry throughout the other two stories. While this is a standalone, reading books two and three may enhance your reading experience.

Trigger Warnings

This book contains mentions of parental abuse (In dialogue and briefly on page), narcissism, self-harm, religious trauma, infertility (not the main characters), Miscarriage (not the main characters), Bondage, cnc, masochism, and a breeding kink. This book is a Dark Spicy Romance Novel and is intended for a mature audience. It may not be suited for all readers. Readers Discretion is Advised.

Other works by Amber Rodriguez

<u>StandAlone</u>
Beautiful Chaos
<u>Springville Trilogy</u>
The Son of a Pastor
The Son of a Ghost
Book 3

BOOK ONE IN THE SPRINGVILLE TRILOGY

THE SON OF A PASTOR

AMBER RODRIGUEZ

1. Prologue

8 years ago

"Taste it," August smirks, just as he smears strawberry icing from his cupcake onto his finger and eating it. We aren't supposed to be out after dark, but my parents are arguing again, and August is the only one I can talk to about it. That led to us sitting in his best friend's truck behind Maxxie's Diner.

"What if I don't like it?" I say, looking up at him. Since the explosion with our parents, we've been hanging out in secrecy and eating sweets. He pauses a moment, swiping icing on his finger again before licking it off. "Just taste it, if you don't like it, I won't bug you about it ever again," He replies reassuringly.

I take a deep breath, swiping icing on the tip of my finger, saying, "Fine." Once the icing hits my taste buds, it's a sweetness overload. My face scrunches up. This is exactly why I deemed I didn't like icing the first time I tried it, it's too sweet, taking the enjoyment away from the pastry.

Once my tastebuds settle, I look over at him, and he's waiting for a response. "I still don't like icing," I reply, finally taking a bite of the bottom side of the cupcake. He laughs as he finishes eating his. Swallowing I continue, "and thanks by the way. For being here with me."

He smirks, "Thanks for being here too." We continue to eat the cupcakes, August finishing off the top halves of mine. It's not much for a celebration but I hope it's nice enough. I ask, "So is this how you imaged spending your seventeenth birthday?" He's only a year older than me and he's so hot.

It's still insane to think I'm actually hanging out with the guy I've had a crush on since last year. Before the chaos with our parents we ran in two different crowds, who would have thought my dad cheating with his mom would have thrown me on his radar. It's still makes me nervous being alone around him.

"It's not how I thought I'd spend today, but I'm glad I'm spending it with you anyway," He smiles, his voice sounding sincere, and I smile back at him. If he tries to go to third base with me tonight, I'm totally letting him.

2. Awkward Reunions

The present

Weddings are supposed to be happy, memorable, and fun. Flowers, Dresses, and Bridesmaids are supposed to be the only thing you want to talk about. But today is none of those things. Today is one of the last few days before I attend the funeral of my freedom.

"Mom, I've tried on at least ten dresses. Will you just pick one?" I complain as I stare at my mother while she talks with the associate holding up two more dresses. She ignores me, of course, so I turn to stomp away into the dressing room.

She comes in shortly after, with two of the same white dress, saying, "Here, Hazel, try the xl on first. Then, we'll stop at Pinky's Hair Salon." She hands me both of the white dresses before leaving. I shake my head knowing I'm only a little piece in her puzzle while she's happy in her own little world.

I sigh, standing up. I hold the 2X dress against my body in the mirror, knowing this one will fit. My natural hair is hidden neatly under my lace front wig, while the jet-black curls of twenty two inches dance just above my elbows.

I strip, staring momentarily at the few tattoos I have mostly in rebellion, but all three have meanings; my first one is of a cupcake located under my right boob. I got it for my twentieth birthday, a reminder of that night with August all those years ago. The second is on the left side of my torso, of tiny black birds, and lastly, a small quote written backward on my right thigh, over healed but damaged skin.

Quickly putting the dress on, I notice how it completely covers my body with its full lace, bell-like sleeves. The lace continues down to my breast, where it meets solid white satin that continues past my knees. This dress hugs my curves ever so slightly, showing off my pear-shaped body and complementing my dark skin nicely.

Originally, I wanted a princess dress with a tiara and everything, but the moment my mother realized I was having fun, she deemed the dress a slut show and unchurch-like.

After judging myself in the mirror, I walk out and resume my position on the black round podium and wait for my mother's response. She smiles clapping her hands together, "Oh my, you look gorgeous, Hazel!"

She smiles, saying, "Give me a spin." She directs me with her finger, and I oblige. She claps once more, "Yes, this is the one! Hazel, dear, be careful taking this dress off and hurry. We still have a few errands to run around town."

I smile in response, and as soon as she turns away, I frown and roll my eyes. She is right, though. This dress is the nicest, but I can't wait to get her out of my hair. The first thing I want to do is have a glass of red wine and hopefully drown in a hot bath.

I quickly but carefully remove the dress and meet my mother at the counter. This bridal shop is just one of the many mom-and-pop shops in Springville. The population here grew a few thousand since the last time we were here, though it is still small settling at just a little over 14,000. It sits just a couple hours outside of a busy city called Va'More, luckily, the tourist prefer to hang over there since it offers more attractions then just a few Forrest trails.

After paying for the dress, we leave the shop to walk only a block away. Surprisingly, there are so many unfamiliar faces, I'm kind of glad I haven't seen anyone I know. You can hear my heels clicking against the pavement as I clutch my black purse.

Walking this long in heels used to have me in tears, but when you have a mother like mine, who cares so much about the opinions of others and nothing about you. Well, you develop a tolerance to pain and an ability to learn fast.

We cross Infront of plenty of flourishing shops, advertising clothes, food, and knickknacks. I forgot how nice it is, seeing proud independent business owners, and not a single name brand business in sight. Next thing you know, we set foot in a familiar setting—Pinky's Hair Salon. My mother used to take me there every other weekend to either get her hair done or mine.

"Sorry, we're about to close," Cathy begins before she looks up, stopping herself, "Carla? Is that you?" Cathy's voice rings old and wise as she calls out to my mom, and my heart melts. She was my safe space growing up and seeing her again after so many years. I didn't realize how much I miss her.

Her gray hair sits just above her shoulders as the tips curl inward, and she's wearing a long red and green kimono. My mother replies quickly, greeting her in a hug, "Cathy, it's so good to see you!"

Cathy turns to look at me in astonishment, "Don't tell me, Hazel?" Her voice pitches at the end as a smile erupts on my face, and she moves to hug me, "My dear God, you've grown into such a beautiful young woman."

"Thank you," I say. She continues, "Well, let me look at you." She twirls me around, and I can't help but laugh. She eyes my long sleeve autumn-colored dress and black tights. "Well, I'm glad to see your mother hasn't been starving you," She smiles approvingly.

My mother butts in, taking a seat in one of the waiting chairs, "Considering that the wedding is in two days, I should have." Both Cathy and I drop our smiles as we look over at her.

Cathy dismisses her and changes the subject, "So, what Pastor Forkhill said is true then, Hazel's going to marry August this Saturday?" My stomach turns at the mention of his name. I haven't seen him since that night at Maxxie's Diner, that was *eight years ago.*

"Yes and thank God for the opportunity," my mother says. She crosses her legs and continues, "Hazel needs her braids refreshed, do you have time?" Cathay turns to me and points to her salon chair on the left side of the building, "I always have time for you, Hazel Grace. Come on, sit."

My mother talks mindlessly on her phone as I fall under the spell of Cathy's skilled hands. She starts by swiftly removing my wig and quickly takes down my braids. She washes my lace and my natural hair. Then she takes her time re-braiding it and laying my lace.

This brings back so many memories from my childhood. By the time she's done, I almost forget the doom that lurks within the next few days. I sigh happily when I can finally stand from the salon chair.

"Thank you so much, Cathy," I say wholeheartedly, and I move to hug her goodbye. "Anything for you, Hazel. Remember, if you ever need me, I'll always be here," She waves me and my mother out the door before I could get any mushier.

We walk back to the parking lot where my mother's white Volkswagen Passat sits, and we quickly get in. When she starts the car, she begins, "We have about forty-five minutes before we have to be at Pastor John's house. As soon as we get back to the hotel, you need to start getting ready, and please take a shower, not a bath. Remember, cleanliness is close to Godliness."

I fight the urge to roll my eyes as I adjust my purse and respond, "Yes, Mother." I would argue and say to each their own, but I'd rather save the energy. In just two more days, this Saturday she'll no longer have a say over me.

We pull in front of our hotel. It isn't top notch or anything, but it's the nicest hotel in town. People only book here for special occasions. I rush out of the car and through the main door, eager to get away.

The inside of this hotel is just as beautiful as the outside. High ceilings and chandeliers. Crisp white floors and gold trims. I hurry to the second floor and into our hotel room; it's a double suite with two rooms and a bathroom. I head into the bathroom, only taking a breath when I've closed and locked the door.

This bathroom is spacious with marbled counters and double sinks. The shower is separate from the tub, with black tile and clear glass walls. The tub is big enough for two people, maybe three. One thing I know for sure is, my mother married my father for love, Everyone else, she married for money.

I put my hair in a ponytail and grab my bathroom bag off the counter before moving to run the bath water. Taking my time, I undress as the tub fills, wrapping my earth-green bonnet around my hair. I savor the moments like this, where I can just be without worry or stress. Just simply being.

When the tub is full, I sink into the almost unbearable heat. Letting it sting as I rest my eyes for a moment. In a few more days, my hopes, and dreams of traveling and seeing the world will come crashing to an end.

I sigh heavily, forcing back the tears and the pain in my chest. I slowly move my left hand over my breast and down my stomach. "Just to take the edge off, I can be quick," I whisper to myself as my fingers stop just above my clitoris. I try to picture what August looks like now, but all I can see is a blurry face, man. After all, I haven't seen him since I was sixteen.

So, I pretend to know what he looks like; maybe his hair grew out, and hopefully, he's tall. I rub my clit between my fingers as I let my fantasy edge me on. I whisper a quiet moan as I adjust my hand to stick a finger inside myself while rubbing my palm against my clit.

Maybe I could like August, if this wasn't forced, if we found each other on our own, we lived in the same small town after all. I work my fingers faster, feeling my orgasm nearing. I try to think of his hands on my body. Working across my breast and around my waist. "Oh God," I whisper just as I'm about to push myself over the edge.

"Knock, Knock!" My mother's voice rings in my ears. My eyes shoot open, and I sit up, whipping my head toward the door. I try to clear my voice, "Yes?"

"Hazel, you need to hurry. We don't want to be late. I've laid out a dress for you in your room, don't make me come back up here." I take a deep breath before sweetening my voice, "I'll be out right now." I wait until I hear her footsteps walk away before I sulk back into the water.

After forcing myself out of the tub and into a towel, I stare at a beautiful mid-length cream-colored knitted tight dress. Although it shows off my curves, it is long sleeve, with a high collar, I compliment it with a gold necklace and matching earrings.

I add on a pair of thick black tights and small black boots. I refresh my make-up and finally remove my bonnet, happy to see the lace still laid and invisible.

As I walk out into the lobby, my mother and Thomas wait, dressed for the occasion. "There she is," He smiles at me as I reach them.

Thomas is my mother's third husband since my father and just like the one before, she has him wrapped around her finger. Time to play nice. "Ready," I say as the car is already out front and waiting.

I can hear my heartbeat in my ears as we sit silently in the car. My mouth runs faster than my mind when I accidentally ask, "Is Dad going to walk me down the aisle?" My mother's shoulder tense at the mention of my father.

Really, I shouldn't want him there, considering what he's done to our family, and I'm really only in this situation because of him. Maybe it's still that small bit of hope he'll rectify the situation and save me from this marriage the day of. Sadly though, deep down, I know that won't happen.

After everything came to light, He left and never looked back. My mother pretends she didn't hear the question as Thomas speaks, "I don't think he will be, but you know I will if you want me to, Hazel." I don't know why I set myself up for heartbreak, but either way, it still hurts when I hear it. "Yes, that'll be fine," I sigh, clutching my purse.

The pastor's house screams wealth as the lawn is cut crisp and lush green, its two-story building is no more than a decade. Thomas helps my mother out of the car, and we reach the doorsteps. My mother says excitedly, as she rings the doorbell, "This is It! Hazel, God help me, be on your best behavior. I need not remind you this is *the* Pastor of Springville."

"Carla, it's only dinner, leave the girl alone," Thomas chastises her just as the doors open. "Welcome!" Pastor Forkhill greets us at the door with a bright smile.

"It's good to see you again, Carla!" He reaches to shake my mother's hand. His salt and pepper hair is short with a neat trim, And the youthfulness in his features makes me question his age. "It's so good to be back in our hometown, John," My mother replies.

She turns to introduce Thomas, "This is my husband, Thomas Hopper, and This is Hazel." John shakes Thomas's hand, "We're happy to have you." He turns to me and grins, "You look lovely, Hazel. Welcome back to town; it's a pleasure hosting you tonight." I smile, "Thank you, Pastor Forkhill. It's good seeing you too."

"Come on inside. Dinner should be ready," He ushers us inside, leading the way to the dining room. A long, beautiful dark wooden dining table stands in the center of the room, seating eight chairs, "Hello, everyone," my mother smiles, looking at Larson: John's oldest son, and his wife, Rachel.

Rachel immediately stands, moving to hug my mother. Her Medium blonde bob cut hair dances with her movement. "Carla, it's so nice to have you back in town!" I smile patiently amazed how everyone oddly looks the same, just older.

"Well, I'm glad to be here," My mother responds, reintroducing Thomas to the table. Rachel turns to me, her blue eyes dazzling me momentarily, "It is so good to see you, Hazel. I have been looking forward to tonight all week long. Come sit beside me." I smile, "It's good to see you too, Rachel."

Rachel is three years older than me, so we didn't hang out much back then, still I allow her to guide me to her seat at the table. When we're all seated, Mother points out, looking at the last two empty chairs, "Will August be joining us for dinner tonight?"

John, sitting at the head of the table, replies reassuringly, "Of course, he should be down any moment." He looks at Larson who's sitting on the right side of Rachel and makes a face but I don't bother reading into it. I'm sitting next to the other empty chair at the foot of the table.

Suddenly Lisa walks in, hands full, and begins setting food on the table, "Dinner's hot, so be careful." I glance at my mother as anxiety and shock run through me. She looks like she's seen a ghost but immediately fixes her face. Did John *stay* with Lisa? After everything she's done, really?

As if my mother can hear my thoughts, she speaks sourly, "Lisa. I didn't expect to see you here." Thomas reassuringly places his hand on my mother's thigh as Lisa takes the seat between him and John.

Lisa answers my mother obliviously, "Well, By the grace of God and prayer. I'm still here. Honey, would you like to say grace?" She leaves it at that as John clears his voice, "Of course, dear. My apologies, Carla, I should have told you beforehand." John turns his head towards the archway that leads to the hall, "August, just in time!"

We all turn to look at August, and my heart nearly skips a beat. There he is, the man I'm supposed to marry. I can finally place details to my blurry vision of him, and God, he's attractive. How long was he standing there for? He stands at an average height 5'8 maybe. His body lean, and defined. He looks good.

His straight brown hair is trimmed on the sides, with a clean-cut taper fade. His voice sounds deep but flat as he responds, "It's nice to see everyone getting along." Finally moving to take the seat on my left, his brown eyes land on me, and I burn under his gaze. As he sits down next to me, he nod towards me, saying, "Hazel."

That's it? I reply quietly, "August." I give him the same attention he seemingly gives me, and I turn to look at the now full table. John smiles happily, "Let us say grace."

Everyone awkwardly moves to hold hands. I place my right hand in Rachel's. I turn to look at August, and he's already eyeing me, his right hand patiently waiting for mine. I look at his hand then back at his eyes before reluctantly setting my hand in his. There's some type of electric current running through me from his touch, I take a deep breath trying to remain calm.

We bow our heads, and John begins saying grace, but I can't focus on his words. He's still with the women who destroyed his family, who destroyed mine. By the grace of God, my ass. I wonder how August feels about it.

I hear everyone say amen before I can reel in my thoughts, rushing the words out quietly. I look at Lisa as she picks up a basket of bread rolls and starts placing some on John's plate and her own. Her chocolate brown hair, laced with grey strands, sits in a neat low bun, stress wrinkles sit on her forehead as she continues piling John's plate.

I watch silently as everyone focuses on making their plates. Rachel steals my attention, "So now that you're back in town, I would love some help at the diner. The owner's name is Maxxie and I'm the only waiter. It would be awesome if you'd come to work with me! If you don't mind the work, I mean."

"Yes, I don't mind," I reply, reaching to pour myself a glass of wine. "Here, let me get that for you," August reaches for the red bottle of Mwenzi wine and my glass. I wait patiently as he fills it, then hands it to me. "Thank you," I say, taking a sip, and he watches me. It's so sweet and smooth, I have to refrain from moan out in pleasure.

"Do you like wine?" he asks, moving to cut his chicken into pieces. I smile lightly, responding, "More than I should." He nods in response before continuing, "Aren't you hungry? You should eat."

"Oh, I'm actually not that hungry," I try to say. I know that I'm lying, considering I've only eaten a bagel today, but I hate eating in front of people, or at least in front of my mother. He moves to stab a piece of his chicken and holds it to my lips, "You should eat, Hazel."

I hear the room fall to a low buzz as I stare at him momentarily. What is his deal? "No, really, I'm okay," I say respectfully.

He pressures me, jokingly, "Well, if you don't eat now, then I'll be forced to cook you a whole meal myself and watch you eat every last bite." What the Hell? Suddenly my mom kicks my foot under the table, which makes me snap my head at her. Is she going to critique me in front of everyone?

I turn my attention back to August and I take a deep breath before moving to bite the meat off of his fork. He watches me, not moving an inch as I begin to chew. The Lemon peppered chicken makes my mouth water as I quickly swallow.

I wait, and it looks like he wants to say something else, but he holds his tongue and continues eating. I reach for my wine again, and it's like everyone resumes their conversations.

3. Games

AUGUST

I almost spit up my drink the day my father told me who I'd be taking to the altar. He thinks marrying Hazel and I will somehow restore the faith of our community. After people found out about my mother's cheating scandal, we lost a lot of church members.

Jaxton, the bastard, he couldn't even face his sins, leaving his wife and daughter to suffer the consequences. It was no surprise they left town a week later.

It's 11 a.m. as I park in front of the church for rehearsal. The cool autumn air sends a brief chill through me as I step outside the car. Looking to my right, I see Carla's car is already here.

By this time tomorrow, I'll be a married man. I laugh at the thought. My father's plan is ridiculous, but his congregation seems to be getting smaller with each passing week. I mean it's not like we *need* the congregation, but he did build it from the ground up, so I don't blame him for wanting to try. I linger a moment more before walking into the church.

Rachel's running the show as she's directing Hazel where she'll be standing and where to face. She writes something on her clipboard as she notices me and says, "Perfect, August, you're right on time!" She nearly runs to grab my arm, pulling me to the front of the Church to stand in front of Hazel.

I look down at her as she's focusing on Rachel's words. "Hello, Hazel Grace," I say, and she looks up at me. "Hi," she squeaks, and I fight back a smile.

Her dress is long-sleeved and mustard yellow, and her breast are emphasized by the way it wraps them. I clear my throat; I'd be a fool to get excited in front of everyone. She is so short compared to me, it's kind of adorable.

Nervously, she looks elsewhere. I probably scared her off, but I didn't like how she wasn't eating last night. Knowing her mother, I am not surprised she carried that trait from our childhood into her adulthood.

"August!" Rachels snaps, getting my attention. "Did you hear me? You'll need to give a brief speech encouraging those who arrive to also attend church on Sunday," she says, writing something down. "Yes, I have it," I say, glancing over at my mother, who's sitting quietly in one of the rows, and Carla sitting a chunk of distance away from her.

The rehearsal continues on like that for the next twenty minutes. Rachel's directing everyone as we move around like chess pieces. Hazel is quiet most of the time, and I can't help but steal glances at her which she responds with a smile or a shy sorry.

I know I keep brushing her hand, feeling her every chance I get. She has a neutral expression on her, too calm, blank, a mask, and I know she's so much more under it.

Finally, Rachel wraps things up, and Hazel quickly darts to the bathroom. "Don't stay up too late, August. I love you," My mother says as she leaves the church. I simply nod at her as I walk up to Rachel and Carla.

"She reminds me of him every day," I hear Carla saying to Rachel, "and I can't stand her because of it." Is she talking about Hazel? I clear my voice which catches their attention. "Oh, August, I didn't see you there. I'm just waiting for Hazel to come from the bathroom," Carla points in the direction Hazel ran to.

"Actually, Carla, I'd love to spend some time with Hazel. After all, we haven't seen each other since we were kids, and I have to lock up," I say as she looks at Rachel.

She tries to hide a smile as she says, "Okay. No funny business, *Mr. Forkhill* God sees everything." I agree, "Yes, yes, he does." They leave the church, and I lock the doors behind them. It feels much calmer now. I head to the front row and take a seat, waiting for Hazel to emerge.

Ten minutes go by, and she still hasn't come from the bathroom. It's against my better judgment, but I decide to go looking for her. As I approach the restroom door, I can hear faint moans, and my dick immediately reacts, pulsing as I hear it again. I open the door slowly stepping inside.

Hazel's sitting against the sink; her tights are down to her ankles, and her dress is pulled up as she angled just enough to snake her hand onto her clit. If this is what God sees every day, he's a lucky man. She moans again. Good God, I breathe to myself. She hasn't noticed me yet, as her eyes are closed. My cock is full-blown hard now, and if I wasn't a gentleman, I swear I'd take her right here and now.

"August," she moans quietly.

Fuck me. Did I hear her right? My cock pulses again, and I move to lean quietly against the door. This is going to give me blue balls if I don't do something. Finally, she opens her eyes, and she gasps, "Oh my God!" She tries to pull her dress down and her tights up.

I shake my head, my voice laced with desire, "Don't stop. You look like you're having fun." She continues to pull up her tights and panties, huffing, "You didn't see that." I smile, moving towards her, "Oh, but I did." She doesn't respond as I stop right in front of her, "Go on, show me that pretty pussy of yours. I promise I won't touch." I smile devilishly.

She hesitates a moment before slowing sliding her fingers back into her panties. She watches me, and a moan escapes her lips just as she touches herself. I praise her darkly, "That's a beautiful sound you make, Miss Grace." I shove my hands in my pockets, as I intend to keep my promise, but my mouth waters at the sight of her.

She looks so beautiful, partially displayed like this. Her eyes don't leave mine and my pants feel tighter as my bulge fills them. My eyes rake her body as I move to lean back against the wall, and her eyes fall to my cock. I watch as her breathing becomes quick and shallow. Looking at her thick two-tone lips,

I wonder briefly how they'll feel around my cock. I could pull my dick out and shove it down her pretty little mouth right now, and I bet she'll let me. My cock throbs at the thought, but I can't. I don't want to ruin her before she's even mine.

Just then, she inhales sharply, "Oh God." She moans as an orgasm washes over her, throwing her head back as she slightly slumps, enjoying the wave.

When she comes down, she removes her hand and readjusts her clothes. Only then does the realization of what just happened hits her face. I calmly walk up to her enjoying her embarrassment more than I should.

She stays still, too embarrassed to look up at me. I gently press my hard cock against her, moving to whisper in her ear, "I'm going to have so much fun with you." I pull back, and her eyes look bewildered.

I have to fight a smile from spreading on my face as a brief image of her tied up and gagged with those same wide eyes flash across my face. I clear my throat, saying, "I told your mother I'd bring you back to the hotel, shall we?" I hold out my arm for her.

She doesn't move before saying, "Please don't tell anyone." I laugh, "Why would I tell anyone what goes on between us?" She seems to relax after hearing this, "This isn't weird to you?" She questions, looping her hand in my arm as we leave the bathroom.

"What? Watching you masturbate inside of God's house?" I tease, and she tries to punch my arm. "That is not what I meant, August. We're getting married tomorrow, and we barely even know each other," She sighs as we approach the main doors of the church.

I reach into my pocket and pull out the keys and unlock the door, "That's not true. I still remember your favorite color and your gag reflex." I say that last part more to myself as I open the door for her, but she hears me anyway. "You are pathetic," She rolls her eyes, pulling away from me.

As she steps outside, I follow her, grabbing her arm and pulling her into me. She struggles for a moment before sighing and looking up at me, annoyed. "I'm sorry, Hazel. But you know we're not strangers. I care about you," I say, completely wrapping my arms around her. She huffs, "Yeah, okay, the only thing you cared about was getting in my pants." I don't respond, knowing that may have been true when we were a couple of teenagers.

She looks around, realizing our close proximity and the fact we're outside of the church, "Let me go, August, before someone gets the wrong idea. We're not married yet." She spits out the last part as I release her from my arms.

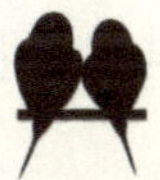

My car's annoyingly recognizable as I pull into Daniel's neighborhood waving and smiling at those who recognize me. I need to stop delaying getting these windows tinted. Soon I pull into his driveway.

He's standing on the porch as I quickly get out of my vehicle. After dropping Hazel off, I stopped by my house to rub one out and change into more comfortable clothes knowing the guys and I are heading out.

"We almost thought you weren't coming, man!" Daniel reaches for a handshake as I approach him. The evening sun hits Daniel's red hair, making it look like fire. "Like I'd miss my own bachelor party. Where's Caleb?" I ask as He follows me through his front door and into the kitchen. Daniel's taller than me, and not as slim, but he's too goofy to be any real damage. "He's in the bathroom," He responds over my shoulder as I grab a beer from the fridge. I quickly crack it open, taking a swing.

"What are we doing tonight?" Caleb asks, emerging from the hall with a beer already in hand. Caleb is taller than me too, but not six foot like Daniel. His hair is in black dreadlocks that go down his back. He's always calm, and laid back, but down for whatever.

I lean against the counter saying, "You guys are supposed to be my best friends, and you didn't plan something? Pathetic." Caleb snickers, taking another sip of his beer, "I have plenty of plans for tonight but there's only so much I can do for you, pastor boy." He finishes his beer and moves to secure his dreadlocks into a ponytail, "Let's go boys, we've got some fuck shit to do." A smile erupts on my face as Daniel, and I chug the rest of our beer and follow Caleb to his car.

"So do you think the whole town will show up to the wedding tomorrow?" Daniel asks from the backseat. I purposefully ignore the text I hear ding on my phone and reply, "That's the goal right." Caleb laughs, "I'm sure you guys will cause a lot of commotion in town." He makes a right into the town's bowling alley.

We're sitting around switching into the provided bowling shoes as I say to Caleb, "You know I thought you had something much more fun in mind." He smiles as we stand walking down to our lane. He responds, "It *is* going to be fun and it's good for publicity, you want the town at the wedding tomorrow and at church on Sunday. Families like to come out on Friday night. Show them you're like family, not just the pastor's boy."

"If you call me that one more time–" I begin. He cuts me off laughing, "Relax, man. Just act normal." He pats my shoulder as Daniel moves to put our names in the system. "Your go," Daniel says to me as the screen lights up with our names.

I pick out a black bowling ball but set it down as my fingers are too big for the holes. I choose a red one that fits my fingers and make my way to the lane. Briefly looking over my shoulder, I notice a few families staring and whispering in shock. Never a dull moment in the public eye.

I swing the ball, rolling it perfectly straight down the lane. It knocks down all of the pins, earring me a strike. Daniel cheers and I hear Caleb clap mockingly, "Yeah, don't get too excited, It's only the first round." I take my seat and It's Daniel's turn.

Caleb asks, "So are we going to talk about her?" I look at him, "Hazel? Do you mean is she off limits? Yes, she is." I look around making sure to speak low so no one else can hear me.

Disappointment flashes on his face as quickly as it disappears, and I take a deep breath closing and opening my hands to keep calm. Of course, he asks if she's in the deck of cards for that kind of game, Hell I don't even know what she's into and I'm not so sure I want to share.

Daniel misses three pins, and I tease, "Come on Daniel, you've got better aim then that." He dismisses me with a shrug as he waits for the ball to come back. Caleb continues our conversation, "What are you going to do about your pet?"

"I'm handing it," I say, knowing that it's a lie. I haven't completely dealt with it yet. "Sure, you are. Well, if not, I'll gladly take her off your hands, besides you know she likes me more," he smirks as he gets up for his turn. Caleb is such an asshole. I reply, "We'll see."

We continue the next hour or so playing, not minding the watching eyes around us.

After we finish the game, we find ourselves back at Daniel's house and quickly parting ways, "I'll catch you guys at the wedding." We say our goodbyes and I make my way home. I finally pick up my phone to see the message I've ignored all day, stating Kim is right where she is supposed to be. Well not anymore.

I pull up to my house that sits right outside of town near a plot of color changing trees. I quickly park in my driveway and get out the car, it's pitch black outside, the only light illuminating from my porch and streetlight.

I unlock the door and immediately see the bible sitting on the coffee table I keep near the door. It's quiet as I take my time settling in, normally I'd relish in these few minutes of anticipation but that's all about to change.

When I finally make it to the bedroom door, I take a deep breath as I open it. There at the foot of the door sits an XL black metal doggie kennel, with Kim inside of it. I give her a sad smile as I close the door behind me, I know she's been in here since she sent me a text earlier. "Kim, I told you this was over weeks ago." I say opening the kennel, not playing our normal game.

"I know but I just wanted one more night with you," She sighs, crawling out and I try to not look at her breast peeking through the lingerie she's wearing. She sits on the bed as I stand in front of her. "This game is no longer ours to play, Kim," I say and her face fills with sadness as she moves to grab her bag. I'll need to get rid of the kennel and change the location of where I keep the spare key.

I sigh, "Caleb asked about you today." Her head perks up at the sound of his name as she pulls a shirt out of her bag. "He did?" she asks as she continues to get dressed.

Caleb and I, even Daniel have shared a handful of women, and even though Kim is mine, *was* mine. I know she enjoys playtime with Caleb. "He did," I respond simply. She sits in thought for a moment before sighing, "I'll miss you." I don't respond as I move to open the bedroom door for her, "Goodbye Kim."

4. Mr. and Mrs. Forkhill (yeah right)

Chaos. That's what this morning feels like. Everyone is everywhere. Excitement and joyfulness rushing all around me. I manage not to cry this morning, but the closer I get to the ceremony, the harder it becomes.

"Hazel, sweetie, eat something light this morning; we don't want any interruptions at the wedding. Oh, I almost forgot! I need to call the florist!" My mother says, rushing out of the hotel's bathroom as I hang the dress on the back of the door. It's sitting in a clear plastic covering. I have a little over two hours before the wedding, and I need the smallest taste of freedom I can get in this town.

I quickly throw on a black pair of leggings and a fitted black shirt. I snag my cell phone and my wireless earbuds and head for the door. I begin to jog, ignoring everyone I pass, with a tunnel vision for the trees. Not slowing down until I've reached the beginning of a familiar trail on the outskirts of town.

I take a deep breath and run. Running like my life depended on it. The path starts off small but widens as I run deeper into the greenery.

My chest begins to hurt as my lungs struggle to fill with air, but I don't care. I welcome the pain. When the overgrowth of grass and bushes become more abundant, I finally slow down to catch my breath, placing my hand over my chest.

My mind immediately thinks about the tattoo just underneath.

Never in a million years did I think I would see August again. Let alone marry him. Would he know the reference? His seventeenth birthday, the day he took my virginity. We went to high school together, but we weren't always in the same world back then.

I pull out my earbuds as a Hozier song fills the quiet space. I lay on the thick grass, closing my eyes and breathing in mother nature. I envy her, forever unbound from the world of law or religion. Against all odds, she prospers in her beauty and freedom.

"Well, this is a lovely surprise."

My head snaps up to see August, shirtless and in gym shorts with sweat gleaning over his chest and forehead. He takes out his earphones as I say, "It's bad luck to the see bride before the wedding." I stand as he approaches me. I try taking a deep breath, cursing myself for not snagging a water bottle from the front desk. He smiles, "I think I'm lucky enough."

Now with both of our earbuds out, the birds surround us in a quiet melody, "Don't they sound beautiful?" He arches an eyebrow, "What does?" I look around us, "The birds, they sound so beautiful when you just stop and listen."

He pauses, closing his eyes and listening to birdies around us, "Sounds peaceful." I agree, and he opens his eyes. Taking a step closer to me he asks, "So is that what you are; a peaceful little bird?" I shrug my shoulders, "I aspire to be like them I guess, but they have something I lack."

I move to check the time and decide to go back to the hotel before my mother calls, "I should go don't want to be late." He watches as I begin to leave, lightly smiling, "Yeah, I should too. See you at the altar."

My mind is hazy and on auto pilot from the moment I walk back into the hotel to the moment I find myself just seconds away from walking down the aisle. "Hazel Marie?" My mother calls me, pulling me from my thoughts. "Hmm?" I respond, realizing I can feel the threads of my dress clinging to my body.

"Thomas is talking to you," She points at Thomas, who I didn't realize is standing on my left side. "I'm sorry," I say turning to him. He smiles at me, "Are you ready?"

He holds his arm out for me as my mother shoves a flower bouquet in my hands and readjust the veil pinned into my bun. I nod as the music starts playing, and we walk out into the aisle. I take a deep breath, here goes the final walk from one cage to another.

I quietly gasp as it looks like the whole town is here. I quickly stare down the aisle at nothing in particular. Plastering a smile on my face, we walk at a steady pace, and I hear my heartbeat thump in my chest.

My face softens as we reach the front of the church, and I notice Cathy smiling at me. She mouths, "So beautiful." I slightly nod, mouthing back, "Thank you," in response, genuinely smiling at her.

Finally, when we stop walking, I meet August's brown eyes and my breath catches in my throat. He's dressed handsomely in a fitted black suit and traditional tie, all evidence of the sweaty man I met this morning gone and replaced by a God.

He's smiling at me as he turns to my stepfather thanking him and taking my hands. Casually he whispers in my ear, "You look breathtaking Hazel." We move to stand under the altar. I'm taken aback by his compliment, but I don't respond. His father stands in between us, with his bible in hand.

I can't help but notice the glee in his eyes. He is actually happy about this, being forced to marry. I bite down on my teeth to refrain from slapping him. Pastor Forkhill begins, "I'd like to thank all of you beautiful people for joining us in witnessing the union of August Grant Forkhill and Hazel Marie Grace." He then begins quoting the bible while talking about the gifts of God and marriage.

I glance around the room as he speaks, the church is beautiful on its own, with its high ceilings and crystal white walls. Six stained glass windows line the walls, with characters from the bible on them. Archways on each side lead off to different rooms and bathrooms. A single chandelier hangs in the center of the isle, and the ceiling is painted with baby angels.

Lastly, at the front, hangs a giant white sculpture of Jesus hanging from the cross. Rachel really didn't really have to put much effort into the décor, simply adding white lilies to the end of each row that lines the isle. I notice Larson is August's only groomsman and Rachel is my only bridesmaid.

I'm so glad my mother didn't force me to say vows, the only good thing is that I just have to stand here and look pretty. My heart rate picks up though when August clears his throat to speak, "Hazel, I know these past few days have been a lot for us to take in, so I'm only going to promise three things to you today." His voice gives me butterflies, sounding hotter than it should.

He continues, "I promise to protect your well-being and spirit, to honor our household, and to be by your side in this walk of life." He squeezes my hands before turning to the crowd, "I personally want to vow to you all in our little town of Springville, to always be a place of peace for you to turn to and to walk in the path of God. I hope to see you all with me, tomorrow morning, here in the house of God."

Everyone briefly claps for him before he turns back to me with our rings. He quickly slips them on and smiles down at me before retaking my hands.

His ring is silver with a black outlining and mine is a simple diamond ring. Unwillingly relief coils through me as I note it's not his mother's ring.

Pastor Forkhill speaks solemnly, "By the grace of God we pray your marriage is prosperous and fruitful. I now pronounce you Mr. and Mrs. Forkhill. You may now kiss the bride." I weakly smile at August feeling a ping of embarrassment. He on the other hand is glowing. A bright smile covers his lips as he pulls me close to him.

He briefly whispers into my ear, "You're mine now." My lips part in shock and quickly he kisses me. My eyes close momentarily and his lips move more passionately than they should as his arms squeeze around me. I can't tell if he's putting on a show or if he's just eager to kiss me. When he pulls away the crowd immediately stands to clap and cheer. My life, now sealed to his.

We begin walking down the aisle smiling and thanking everyone for coming. The crowd follows behind us as rice is thrown in the air once we make it out the doors. A small black car, with *Just Married* written on the back window awaits us. Jesus, they went all in didn't they.

"Thank you all again, I hope to see you all at the reception," August says waving one last time before opening the passenger door. My eyes widen briefly at his words before I resume smiling as he helps me in. My mother didn't tell me about an after party.

He makes his way to the driver's side and quickly gets in. He takes a deep breath before smiling at me. "And the fun begins," he says as he fishes out his keys.

I refrain from rolling my eyes as I say, "You don't have to pretend anymore August, it's just us here." We're still being watched as he starts the car and puts it in drive, "Hazel, give me a little credit, you think I'm pretending with you?"

"Yes, I do," I say annoyed as the car begins to move. I look away from him towards the window, "I understand putting on a show for them, I understand public image and everything but please spare me the bullshit." I refrain from looking at him as I watch the passing of stop signs and buildings. He speaks calmly, "I meant what I've promised to you today. I won't fake anything with you. Unless you want me too of course."

I look back over at him still annoyed and he's smiling, "Wipe that God awful smile off your face or I swear I'll punch you August." He stops at a stoplight and erupts into laughter, "Oh I'd like to see you try." He takes a deep breath, "You know you're quite upset to be a newlywed bride, why'd you agree to marry me if you aren't happy about it?"

I turn back to face the window, not replying to him. He can't know that my mother planned this, to be-wed the pastor's son to get back into the grace of the town, all so she can move here with her freshly retired rich husband, free of judgement and as icing on the cake; free from me.

As far as he knows, my mother simply thinks we're a match made in Heaven, and his father just so happens to agree. The light finally turns green, and we continue the ride in silence until we arrive at the building of our reception party.

He parks the car in the back of the building turning off the ignition as we unclick our seatbelts. "Ready?" he asks. I take a deep breath, "ready as I'll ever be." I plaster a smile on my face as he gets out of the car to open my door. As he helps me out, he says, "Rachel said your reception dress is in the back room."

He shuts the door behind me, keeping my hand in his as we walk into the building and towards the back room, "I'll wait out here for you, take your time." He opens the door for me. "Okay" I respond briefly as I step inside, closing the door behind me.

The room is small, with tan texture walls and wooden floors. A makeup table is off to my right along with a white chair. The dress is hanging directly in front of me, near a full-length body mirror. It's a silky white, body-con, mid-length, square neck dress. I quickly move to take off my wedding dress and the veil. Once I've slipped it on, it hugs my body, showing off my curves, and complimenting my figure. My stomach is visible, but who doesn't like a little extra fluff.

I smile to myself, liking the way I look. It stops right above my knees, still showing off my white heels. I decide to take out the bun, letting my curls flow to give a more casual look. I quickly brush down my hair, checking again to make sure my lace is still laid. The ring on my left finger catches my attention, and I take a deep breath, officially married at the great age of twenty-four.

When I'm finally happy with my appearance, I head to the door. As I open it August turns around and his eyes widen briefly before he smiles, "and just as I thought you couldn't look any more breath-taking." I smile, "Thank you." He holds out his arm saying, "Shall we?" I look up at him for a moment, I should be nice, he's being really nice so it's only fair.

"Let's do it," I loop my left arm into his right, and we head towards the main hall. As soon as we come into view, people cheer and clap for us, the crowd is not as big as it was at the church, but still significantly large. There are dozens of beautiful white lilies all around the room.

Dinner tables line the walls of the room, clearly outlining a dance floor in the middle. There's a food buffet table and my stomach growls at the sight. The DJ at the front of the room turns the music down to introduce us, "You guys please give it up for the official Mr. and Mrs. Forkhill!" Everyone claps louder in cheers. We smile and wave, my eyes not landing on anyone in particular. The DJ continues, "Mr. and Mrs. Forkhill can we get an encore for your beautiful guest, go on and spread the love!"

I look at August, making sure to show my pearly whites, and he smiles down at me, pulling me close and dipping me into a kiss. Our kiss is short but there's still the same fire as before. We hear the crowd go nuts as he pulls me back up, placing his right hand on my lower back. The DJ yells, "Beautiful! The towns new love birds everybody! Don't forget to stop at the buffet table for every-thing from deviled eggs, mac n cheese, and dare I say turkey sliders, Enjoy!" He then plays upbeat background music.

People begin to socialize, and my mother im-mediately walks up to us, "Well done Hazel, You guys look absolutely beautiful together!" I respond dryly, "Thank you mother." She smiles at August,

"You better take good care of her, you hear, she is my only little girl after all." August smiles back at her and pulls me close to him, "Oh I intend too." She turns back to me, "Well I let you lovebirds be." She moves to kiss my cheek and I still, allowing her too.

I smile at August embarrassingly and suddenly his parents walk up to us. His fathers in the middle of finishing off a turkey slider and the smell makes my stomach rumble again. "Welcome to the family Hazel!" Pastor Forkhill says while dusting off his hands. "Thank you, Pastor," I say respectfully.

"Please, you can call me John," he smiles before turning to August, "Congratulations!" His mother begins to say, "We are so very proud of you, son. Hazel we're so happy you're a part of our family now!" I force a smile, "Thank you. I actually need to use the bathroom, excuse me."

I lie, quickly dismiss myself, heading towards the buffet table. There's a bottle of red wine and I couldn't be happier as I pour myself a glass. Taking a sip, I sigh and move to the food. I just need something to hold me until this is over, I reach for two deviled eggs and quickly eat them before taking another sip of my wine.

I take another deep breath and Cathy walks up to me. "There you are!" she says excitedly. She pulls me into a hug with one hand, "you look so beautiful Hazel. I am so happy for you." I set down my glass, "Thank you, I'm so glad you made it."

She says, "I wouldn't miss it for the world dear." Pulling a gift bag from behind her back she continues, "I brought you a little something, Now I know I was supposed to put it near the other gifts, but I wanted you to see it." She hands me the bag and I thank her again as I take it.

Opening it up, I pull out a jar of a home-made dry herb tea mixture. Before I can respond Cathy says, "it's a natural fertility blend. Now, I know they have those pills and things, but I love a good ole natural remedy. I know when you were younger you used to always tell me you wanted a big family, so I hope this helps." I refrain from dropping my jaw as I smile and thank her. She gave me a gift based on the mind of a 12-year-olds fairytale.

I put the jar back into the bag. She smiles, reaching for it, "Here, now I'll go set it near the other gifts." She takes it adding, "Oh, I almost forgot, Justin is here too. Go say hi if you get the chance." My eyes widen at the familiar name, "He is? Where is he?" I glance up at the room and she continues, "He's at the DJ booth dear." I thank her before quickly heading to the DJ booth. The DJ looks up and as I approach, he takes off his headphones, "Hazel!"

"Oh my God Justin!" I move to hug him. "I didn't even recognize you!" I say in pure shock as we both step back to admire each other. His pearly whites gleam against his darkskin and his black poofy afro I remember from our childhood has been cut to a proper fade. His face has matured since I last saw him, but he still has those dark black eyes.

His voice is deeper than I remember as he says, "Look at you all married now!" I jokingly punch his arm, "Oh stop!" His face is still pretty, I'll give him that. "So have you been in Springville all this time?" I ask putting my hands on my hips. "Yeah, I've been here, you know helping ma out with the salon, as she gets older some things aren't as easy, so I stayed to help." he says shyly. That's so selfless. I say, "Well, it's good that she has you."

"Hazel, baby, there you are." I frown turning my head as I hear August calling me, why is he calling me that? Isn't it a little too soon? "August, hi, I was just catching up with Justin, a childhood friend," I say as he steps beside me now with a glass in his hand. "Well, aren't you going to introduce us?" August asks.

Justin cuts in, "oh no need, I remember you from junior year, well it was your senior year. You ran the baseball team fundraisers." August smiles brightly at him, "Well it's nice to meet you again Justin, and thank you for being our DJ. The music has been great so far." August raises his glass to Justin before turning to me, "Can I take you to meet someone?"

I nod my head before saying to Justin, "Well it was great seeing you; I hope to see you again." I wave as August starts to pull me along. He finishes his glass and asks, "Would you like some more wine?" I won't say no to that, "Yes please."

August looks like he's trying not to smile as he guides me to get drinks. "Who are we supposed to be meeting?" I ask once we reach the table, and he begins filling our drinks. "We'll meet them later, I'd actually like to call it a night, I want to take you home Hazel." He says handing me the glass. "Home?" I repeat feeling heat rise to my cheeks. "Yes, our place," he says as if our and we are normal to us. "Okay," I say simply. I mean it's not like I have a choice, we're married now.

5. Brats

AUGUST

After we finish our glasses of wine, I waste no time getting Hazel out of there. The sun sets in the sky during the drive home. "So, are we going to your place, or did your daddy buy you a brand-new house just for you and your wife?" She speaks sarcastically. I tsk at her, "and the fire is back." I briefly look over at her before continuing, "We're going to our house, formally known as my house."

I catch her rolling her eyes from my peripheral vision and I grip the steering wheel. She would have earned herself a spanking, if she was my sub but she's not so I've got to keep it together.

I turn onto the street of my house just as I hear her stomach growl and she immediately apologizes. "Did you eat at the reception?" I ask. "Why do you care?" She snaps. I grip the steering wheel tighter. "Because you're my wife now Hazel, that's why I care." She laughs saying, "I bet you get a kick out of saying that one huh."

I park in front of the house as the night hides everything but the porch light. "You are acting like I am an enemy," I sigh, clutching the keys in my hand. She opens the door to get out of the car, "Yeah well tough luck." Spankings, yep if nothing else, we need to establish having her ass popped.

I take a deep breath running my hands through my hair before getting out of the car and following her to the door, "If you dislike me so much, why did you agree to marry me, Hazel!?" I don't mean to yell, but I do, and she looks around as if worried who can hear. "Lower your voice," she demands. "Tell me?" I reply ignoring her request. She sighs, "Can you just open the damn door August?" So many different ways I could punish her little mouth. I move to do as she asks before I do what cock is begging me to.

She walks in first and I shut the door behind us. I begin loosening my tie, "I won't repeat myself again, Hazel Grace." She glares at me for using her last name, well previous last name. "You want to know the big secret, August? I didn't want to marry you! But you know my mother, right? oh wait you don't, well that dear mother of mine doesn't actually like you, or me for that matter. All she wants is to get back in good graces with the town while getting rid of me, and your father fell for it!" She explains dramatically, pitching and pausing at the right moments.

I laugh. Here I thought my dad was the only one trying to scheme. She looks at me likes she's seeing a ghost, "You're a lunatic, aren't you?" I collect myself quickly, "I guess the both of our parents are going to Hell then." She frowns in confusion, and I continue, "My dad responded to your mom about the marriage proposal because he thought unifying the two households that brought disgrace on Gods house, his words not mine, would somehow rectify the situation and regain the trust and loyalty of the community." After absorbing that information her face softens, "yeah, both of our parents are going to Hell."

After calming down, she finally moves to sit on the living room couch, and I follow her. I'd like to think my house looks nice. It's a two-bedroom, one-bathroom modern home but the way she's making faces at the couches and the décor has me questioning myself. She relaxes, sighing, "I hope you don't mind me asking but why did your dad stay with your mom? After everything came to light?"

I sit beside her, "Truthfully, I don't know. I'd like to think it's because he loves her and they've built so much here in Springville, he probably didn't want to throw it all away." At least that's what I like to tell myself.

She looks away a moment before saying, "I haven't seen my father since that day. I haven't seen him in eight years. He could be dead for all I know." There's no point in me calling out what a piece of shit father she has, I'm sure she already knows that. So, I try to comfort her by placing my hand on her thigh, and she looks at me with glossy eyes, "You're mine now Hazel, okay, I'm here for you."

She laughs weakly, "You still want to go through with this, knowing it's a load of crap?" I smile at her, "I don't believe in divorce." She blinks away her blurry eyes, "So what are you a die-hard Christian? Do you live and breathe the Bible?" I laugh again, "No, it's more like guide-lines." Knowing some of the games I like to play, die-hard Christians condemn me to Hell.

"I'd like to get undress, and shower, can you point me to the bathroom?" she says standing. I point down the hall and she walks past me, my eyes linger on her beautiful round ass, and I fight the urge to smack it. I clear my throat, "It's on your first left."

"Thanks. My suitcase is still in the trunk. Do you mind grabbing it for me?" She asks over her shoulder. "Sure," I respond watching her walk down the hall and disappear into the bathroom. I quickly grab my keys and head out to the car.

I haul her dark green suitcase back into the house, I debate about leaving it in front of the bathroom door for a moment before I decided to knock. "Come in" she yells. "Here's your suitcase," I open the bathroom door not sure what to expect but I definitely didn't expect her to already be naked in my clear glass wall shower.

Her hair is braided to one side, and the water is sliding down her curves, giving her skin a light shine. My dick throbs at the sight of her. She turns around and immediately, I see black ink right under her breast, her side, and on her thigh. "Can you hand me my body wash out of the inside pocket please?" I do as she asks, walking over her yellow bottle of body wash. She opens the glass door and my eyes shoot to her breast, my mouth waters with desire as I hand it to her. Being up close I can see the tattoo under her breast is a cupcake.

My eyes shoot to hers, but I say nothing. That's got to be a coincidence, right? "I'm going to go change," I say dismissing myself as I realize I'm still in my suit and everything's feeling too tight right now.

After I take an excessive amount of time to change, I hear Hazel moving around in the kitchen. As I emerge from the hall, I see her wearing a long sheer black nightgown with matching panties. Is she trying to get fucked tonight? With all her Bratting today I'm utterly surprised but she must know that's not how brats get rewarded.

"What are you making?" I ask. She doesn't turn around as she responds, "Just a quick grilled cheese." She's already transferring it to a plate as I move to grab a glass out of the cabinet for some water. I hear her move to sit at the table as I move to the fridge to fill my cup.

I walk over to join her and see she's not wearing a bra underneath, Keep it together August. "If I didn't know any better, I'd say you're asking to be fucked," I say before taking a sip of my water. She takes another bit of her food before says, "Who says I'm asking." I smile at her, setting down my glass, "You know in my world we have names for girls like you. You are a brat." She laughs and casually says, "Oh really, guess I'll need a brat tamer then." My eyes widen at her response, "What do you know about brat tamers?"

"What do you know about taming brats?" She throws back at me, no longer interested in her food. "See there it goes again," I laugh collecting my glass and taking it to the sink. Truthfully, I lack in that department, I much prefer submissive little pets, "I don't deal with brats." She gets up tossing her unfinished food in the trash and makes her way towards me, "That's too bad Mr. Forkhill because you just married one."

She sets her plate in the kitchen sink before leaving the room. I smirk after her, I'm either going to be a happy man or a miserable one.

After I wash our dishes, I find her sitting on the couch in the living room scrolling on her phone, when I walk in, she asks, "So do you want me to sleep in here or…" She trails off unsure. "We just got married, you really think I'm going to make you sleep on the couch?" I shake my head, but she doesn't respond. I hold out my hand, "Come on, let's go to bed."

She clicks off her phone and gets up walking towards me but passes up my offered hand, heading straight for the hallway. I smirk, shaking my head once more, God help me. I check to make sure the house is locked up before following her. I stop in the doorway to let her explore the room.

My room Is relatively large, with the king-size bed sitting against the middle of the right wall. A black wooden dresser sits at the foot of the bed, as well as a dark leather chest ottoman. She runs her hands on the top of my metal bar bed frame crossing in front of the door to the closet on the left side of the wall. She glances at the two black end tables and only the left side has a table lamp. She settles a frown upon the bed set.

"Well, do you approve?" I ask. "It's industrial looking but nice although this bedding is so thin, you should definitely get thicker blankets now that it's the cold season." She says pulling back the blankets. I shrug my shoulders, finally turning off the light switch and moving to the bed, "I get hot easily." She quickly settles on the left side of the bed but asks, "Do you prefer a side?" I shake my head, settling on the right side, "Not tonight I don't."

I can feel her uncertainty as she lays close to the edge of the bed, so I pull her into me, surprising her, making her let out a little squeak. She's thick no doubt but she feels like a perfect fit in my arms.

Once she settles against my chest I speak quietly into her ear, "The tattoo under your breast, Is that *my* cupcake?" She hesitates a moment before she responds, "Maybe."

My dick pulses at the thought of her marking a memory of me onto her. Maybe she's not so upset about this arrangement as she lets on, "Do they have meanings?" She whispers, "Yes." My arm rests across her waist but I'm itching to run my fingers along her body, to learn her every curve. But I can't, not until we at least discuss hard limits. I clutch my hand into a fist and wish her goodnight.

6. A Midnight God

I wake to an empty bed. I look up at the little red light coming from the rectangle digital alarm clock; it shows 9:33am, I believe church starts at 11:15a.m. I get up and notice August brought my luggage into the room, I move to open it but none of my clothes are inside. I walk out into the hall and the morning breeze makes my nipples hard as I look around for August.

Yesterday, I was too busy being upset to notice how nice his house really is. Modest and industrial looking, similar to his bedroom, but still nice. I hear rustling coming from the kitchen and I find him shirtless in a pair of grey sweatpants. Oh, dear lord.

"Morning," I say breathlessly, from the entrance of the kitchen.

He turns around grinning. "Good morning, coffee?" He asks as he pours himself a cup. "Sure," I say, crossing my arms over my breast, still cold from the thin gown. He pours me a cup and walks it over to me. "Where are my clothes?" I ask, still trying to keep my nips covered as I reach for the cup. "I put them up for you," He responds, standing close in front of me.

"So, you wake up and have coffee every morning?" I ask to make conversation before taking a sip. "After my run, yes, I enjoy a cup or two." I take another sip quickly glancing down at his pants before responding, "That's nice." He smirks, "Like what you see?" I set the cup down on the counter ignoring him, "I need to get dressed."

I begin to leave, but he follows me into his bedroom. "Expecting a free show?" I say, finally turning around to face him as we stop in the room. He shrugs his shoulders, "Just showing you where your clothes are, but if you're offering."

He opens the closet door, "I left a small space for my suites. Otherwise, the closet is basically yours." He points to the dresser continuing, "And for now, the left side dresser has the rest of your clothes, I've ordered you a dresser, but it won't be here until Tuesday." I thank him, and he grabs a random suit from the closet as he lingers a moment eyeing me, before leaving the room.

I take a deep breath and quickly decided what to wear. I settle on a simple black pencil skirt and tan-colored long-sleeve. After doing light make-up, I finish the outfit with small gold bird shaped earrings, and short cream-colored heels.

Already dressed, August knocks lightly before slowly opening the door, I turn to face him. He slowly looks over me, head to toe. "Well, you like?" I ask, giving him a spin. I swear I see a flash of a different light in his eyes, but he blinks it away. Clearing his throat he asks, "Are you ready?" I sigh, slightly disappointed. Nodding my head, I grab my phone and small purse. I swear on the car ride over I feel the burning holes of his stare but every time I glance at him his eyes are stiff on the road.

We arrive five minutes before the service starts and August finally looks at me as he turns off the ignition. "You ready?" He questions with a smile. I unbuckle my seat belt snapping at him, "You keep asking that." He shakes his head unoffended but doesn't respond as he gets out of the car.

He calmly moves to open my door, and I roll my eyes before setting my hand in his. We walk into the church, and I have to force a wide smile on my face to keep from dropping my jaw. There is no one here. Like okay eleven or twelve people are here, but holy cow that's next to nothing. Immediately I realize just how badly our parents ruined the church.

We walk to meet his brother at the front row, this church is meant to seat well over 60 people. I'm still in shock as I greet Rachel, "Hi, how are you?" She smiles and reaches for a hug, "I'm doing good I'm glad you guys made it. You're both helping me with the food drive after church, right?" I nod my head, "Of course Rachel."

Somehow, I feel bad for them. When we were younger the church used to overflow with members, always having to sit packed like a can of sardines. When Pastor Forkhill finally appears at the podium, everyone takes a seat.

I'm sitting between Rachel and August when he places his right hand on my left thigh. I don't know why it sends a bolt of electricity straight to my core, I take a deep breath and fail miserably to pay attention.

After the service ends his family stays to thank the people for coming. "Thank you, we hope to see you next week," Pastor Forkhill says grinning at a single mother and her son. When she leaves, he finally turns to August who's been doing the same, "Son, will you be joining us this evening?" Dread fills me at the thought, but I don't let my reaction show on my face as Rachel cuts in, "Actually Pastor, he and Hazel agreed to help me with the food drive." She smiles at us before turning to Pastor Forkhill.

I mentally thank her for the unintentional save. Pastor Forkhill responds, "Ah, yes well you guys have fun with that. You mother and I are supposed to be helping with youth bible study today, but perhaps another day then."

He smiles again dismissing himself and August says to Rachel, "When do you need us there? I'd like to change before then." Rachel speaks to the both of us, "Well I'd love it if you guys could head over there now, there's a lot more people already lined up then we expected, Larson will need help setting up as quickly as possible."

August turns to me, "Are you okay with that?" I regret not packing a pair of more comfortable shoes, but I'll be fine. "Of course," I respond simply. August turns back to face Rachel, "We'll follow you then."

I feel a little intimidated by the line of people waiting for a hot meal, but I'm also excited to help. The sun isn't shining but it's not cold, so the people are happily waiting. August and Larson get the set up done rather quickly and before we know it, we've got a little serving line going that works quite well.

August is socializing with people waiting in line and I'm simply handing out drinks. A short man and his two kids walk up, and Rachel quickly serves them a pre-made bowl of spaghetti and foil wrapped garlic bread each.

The man speaks, "What do you say kids?" His little ones respond in sync, "Thank you Rachel." She smiles at them. The sight warms my heart as they move towards me. Cathy wasn't wrong, a big family was once a dream of mine.

"Thank you for coming," I smile, speaking kindly and hand them each a water bottle. They thank me in return and the cycle happens like that for the next fifteen minutes until I glance up and see August frowning in front of a particular girl.

I watch her body language around him and it's oddly stiff. As if she's waiting to follow any given order. They exchange a few words and August walks over with a frustrated look on his face. It rubs me wrong, but I shake it away smiling at the next person.

I hear August's footsteps before I see him. "Can I help you?" He asks as if I'm not simply handing out bottled water. "Sure," I reply scooting over as he grabs some water to pass out. I'm all too aware of how close we are as the same girl makes her way to the front.

When her face meets mine, she smiles but it doesn't reach her eyes, "Nice to meet you Mrs. Forkhill." The name sounds so foreign to my ears I almost laugh. Before I can respond though August cuts in, "Hazel baby, this is an old friend, Kim. Kim, this is *my wife*." It's not lost upon me how he is using his words.

They were most definitely not just friends. "Well, it's nice to meet you Kim," I flash her a bright smile while handing her a water bottle continuing, "How'd you meet August?" Her lips press into a thin line, she smiles but her eyes are not so welcoming. She grabs the bottle and says, "Well I don't think it's my place to-" She cuts herself off, as she looks at August. Her defensive demeanor washes away in an instant.

Quickly she follows up with a brief goodbye and hurries away. What the Hell was that? I look over at August who's handing out water as if he missed the whole transaction. I hold my tongue and resume handing out water, making a mental note to probe later.

I'm happy at how fun it was helping Rachel, but now we're all packed up and saying goodbyes, the sun has set, and the cold has finally crept up on us. "Well, now you have my number so let me know when I can drop off those gifts from your wedding!" Rachel says as she hands my phone back to me. "Will do! See you later!" I say walking fast-pace to August's car.

He already has the heater on, so I'm grateful once I close the door and the warmth surrounds me. I take a deep breath finally wanting to talk about earlier, "So are you going to tell me about Kim?" He doesn't even flinch when I say her name, instead throwing the car in reverse then in drive.

So, I wait. We pull up to a stoplight and he still has his eyes on the road. I roll my eyes and look outside. I need to come up with a plan because clearly, I can't be with this man. Falling into my own mind I'm startled when he finally speaks, "Kim was my sub." I look back over at him, and he steps on the gas as the light turns green. Was he really sitting on whether or not to tell me that?

He makes a left and although I don't have the path memorized, I assume we're going home.

He continues, "Do you know what a submissive is?" I reply, "Yes, I've heard the term." Blindly obedient servants, who let men do whatever they want to them. If that's what August expects of me, he's got another thing coming. "So, is that what you expect of me, to be at your every beck and call and worship at your feet?" I ask and he stops at an intersection.

He smirks, "As tempting as that sounds, I don't think you could be an obedient sub if you wanted to." He's definitely right about that but for some reason it stings when he says it. "I've been an obedient daughter my whole life. I'm tired of being obedient." He presses the gas again.

August looks over at me still smiling, "Good thing I didn't marry you for your obedience then." We make a left into an area I think I recognize. He says, "I want you to choose a safe word, I'm not sure what you have or have not experienced but I'd like us to start there. Are you okay with that Hazel?"

Finally, I recognize the road to the house. Safe words are usually reserved for unsafe acts which makes me think he wants to do bad things to me. The question is do I want that too? I carefully respond, "So if I use a safe word, everything stops. No matter what."

He repeats reassuringly, "Yes, No matter what." The car slows as we get closer to the house. He smiles, "What's your safe word Hazel?" It doesn't take me long to think. I whisper almost embarrassingly, "Cupcakes." His smile turns into a grin as we finally come to a full stop. "Do you trust me?" he asks, turning off the car and unbuckling his seat belt. I nod my head suddenly afraid to use my voice. The energy in the car shifts.

I watch as August moves to run his hand first on my right thigh then up my body to my breast causing heat to flood inside me and a gasp to escape my lips. When I look up at him, He's got this dark mischief smirk on his face that sends butterflies to my core and exhilaration to my chest, but if he thinks he's getting in my panties that easily, he's got another thing coming.

Without another thought, I quickly unbuckle my seatbelt and open my side door. Hurrying out, I glance at the darkness of trees in front of me. If he wants me, he's got to catch me first. I debate on taking off my heels but then I hear his car door slam and that thought goes out the window. Oh well.

I move as quickly as my shoes allow. My skirt begins to rise up my thighs as I run into the darkness hoping I don't trip over my feet. These trees aren't too thick or too tall, but still thick enough for me to hide behind. Somehow, I don't think hiding is in my best interest.

I don't dare look behind me, but I can feel my chest beginning to burn and my feet beginning to sore. I haven't run into a tree yet but I'm desperately getting tired. I decide to stop for a break, trying my best to keep quiet as I take deep breaths. The bark against my back feels rigged and the cold air burns my lungs.

After my pulse calms, I try to listen for his footsteps, but I hear nothing. I wait a few seconds more before I hear his voice all around me saying, "Little Bird." His voice is singsong-ish and taunting.

I need to move; I can't let him win that easily. I decide to run to my left, but I trip over an overgrown root sticking out of the ground, catching my fall with my hands, the impact isn't too painful.

Typical. I curse under my breath and turn, moving to sit up. Dusting off my hands I'm startled to see August standing in front of me. "Hello, Little Bird," He smiles his usual smile, but his eyes still have the darkness in them which has every hair on my body sticking up. Somehow the lighting from the moon makes him look Godlike and I swallow as I try to squeeze the heat growing between my thighs.

Still standing above me, he asks, "What's your safe word Little Bird?" I respond quickly still full of adrenaline, "Cupcakes." He smiles as he squats down in front of me, his fingers begin trailing up my thighs, the coolness of his touch earns a gasp from me. This was too fucking easy for him, I should give him more of a fight, but the thoughts in my mind scramble as he says, "I want to do so many naughty things to you, Hazel baby." I feel his fingers reach my inner thighs causing me to shiver, I should not be as turned on by this as I am.

He smiles, "Would you like that?"

If my body could speak, she'd say yes in a heart-beat, but I whisper breathlessly, "Not in a million years." I try to get up determined to run again, but he throws himself over me, pushing my body into the ground, and pinning my arms above my head. His face is now inches from mine as I try to wiggle my arms free cursing myself for not being strong enough. Faster than I'd like to admit I'm out of breath and my chest rises and falls between us.

His tsks shaking his head, "No more running, don't want to hurt those precious feet of yours." I register how he's now nestled in between my legs and the feeling of his growing bulge against me, I say, "Is this how you like your women? Tethered by your grasp and unable to move?" He smiles still looking like a midnight God, "Would you like me to let you go?" I ponder a moment; I could stop this all with one word. Making it so we'd go back to the house, and I'd probably make him sleep on the couch for good measure, but my pussy's too wet for that.

I say nothing and my silent omission sends him into a frenzy. He gathers my wrist in one hand

and his mouth attacks my neck in a mixture of wet kisses and soft bites, a quiet moan leaves my lips as the cold chases every spot he marks. His free hand quickly moves down my body finding my clit above my panties rubbing softly.

I moan again, still unable to move under him and he gloats, "That's what I thought." He moves my panties to the side and barely presses a finger into my pussy, pleased to find my heat, "Already wet for me? And here I thought you couldn't be a good girl." I want to roll my eyes at him but before I can, he presses another finger deeper inside me causing my breast to rise against his chest.

I can feel the hardness of his dick on my leg as he rubs it ever so slightly. He moves to hold himself up, finally releasing my wrists and looks at me, "I want to hear those pretty moans baby." As he speaks, he begins slowly pumping his fingers into me causing me to give him exactly what he wants. "August," I moan his name quietly and I feel his cock pulse against me. "That's right," As he speaks his pace quickens and I curse at how in control he's being while trying to get me to come undone.

I feel that need deep inside me and no way do I want him to reach his goal, I whine, "Please stop." He smiles that leg shaking smile, "Oh but I don't think you want me to." His actions are opposite his words as he quickly removes his fingers and I gasp at the loss of contact.

I watch as he begins to lick those same fingers moaning from the taste of me, my eyes widening at the sight. Jesus, but it only turns me on more. In seconds he's leaning back over me, moving my skirt up more and reaching to pull out and line his cock with my pussy. I feel the heat of his tip and he whispers in my ear again, "Tell God how much you love this cock."

"What?" I begin to reply in confusion, but he slams into me, not giving me a second to adjust to his size, I cry out throwing my head back and my arms around him. "Oh my…" I begin but he only pauses for a second before he pulls out and does it again. "Fuck baby," I hear him moan as his dick fills me up setting off all my nerves. It's too much, too big, it's like I feel him everywhere. I take a deep breath trying to allow my brain to catch up with my body but that's clearly not his goal.

He begins pounding into me rhythmically and all I can do is moan and try to hold on. It's like the cold intensifies every inch of him, coating the pain in pleasure. His left hand finds my clit again, "Look at you, being a good girl and taking every inch of me." His praise makes me clench around him, earning myself a low Godly moan. His voice sounds just as good as his cock feels, and I relish in it.

His pace doesn't waver as he matches a rhythm with my clit and pleasure coils inside me. "Oh, yes!" I breath out feeling that familiar climb. "Fuck baby you sound so beautiful." He praises again and my body responds. Holding onto him I feel myself about to shatter, "Please, don't stop. August, I'm so close!"

Normally this is the part where a guy ruins it because they get too excited but again his rhythm doesn't fault and soon enough, I'm falling over the edge, "Oh!" I momentarily stop breathing and that delightful high washes over me. Still going he praises me, "That's it baby, come all over me."

I take a deep breath still dazed from the high and he moans, "You feel so fucking good on my cock

Little Bird." Still pounding into me, I feel his stroke waver, so I respond, "Come for me August, please come." In a few more strokes he does. I gasp as I feel the warmth of his cum inside of me.

He strokes out every drip before pulling out. "Fuck," he breaths out, collapsing on top of me, and my hands automatically reach to run my fingers in his hair. I feel his cum seep out of me as he takes a moment to come down from the high. When he does, he leans up saying, "Let's go get you cleaned up."

7. My Little Bird

AUGUST

She's quiet on the walk back to the house. I know her feet are sore, and she's covered in dirt and my cum. Once inside I immediately take her to the bathroom. My cocks stirs as I think about her naked in the shower, though I was just inside her. I can feel her silence yelling at me as she watches me turn on the water.

"Something bothering you, Hazel?" I ask, letting the water run under my hands as I adjust the temperature. "We should talk about birth control," she says, and I guess I'm a little surprised that's on her mind. "So, you're not on birth control?" I confirm moving the handle of the facet to be a bit hotter. She replies, "No, the pills make me nauseous, and I'm too overweight for the patch." I frown momentarily, Hazel may be thick but she's not overweight, she's perfect.

When I turn to face her, she's leaning on the counter near the sink, staring at the floor as she rubs her right arm in uncertainty. I move to stand in between her legs moving her chin to look up at me, "I'm not against pulling out." I smile and she laughs a little, "So no condoms?" I tease, "I'll wear one if you want me too, but you *can* slurp me down if you'd like." She laughs harder now, "We'll see how strong your pull-out game is."

Her bird shaped earrings glisten in the light as she watches me. "It'll be as strong as you'd like it to be." I begin moving my hands to the hem of her shirt and pull upwards, "However, I enjoy it being terribly weak." She rolls her eyes as she allows me to remove her shirt and bra, revealing those beautiful round tits of hers. Then I move to pull her skirt and panties off, once she's completely nude, my dick throbs at the thought of filling her again.

She looks vulnerable but she doesn't turn from me, allowing me to drink up her beauty. My eyes trail down to the tattoo on her left side. I smirk at the black birds, knowing her nickname is suiting. I look at the tattoo on her thigh, which looks like backwards writing, but my eyes widen at the scares it covers.

I drop to my knees to touch them. She flinches at the contact, "Don't worry I don't do that anymore." Believing her but still wanting to be clear I say, "You will never harm what *belongs to me,* again, Hazel." I move to kiss the scares, "or you will be punished." She gasps at my response, moving away from me, "You do not get to tell me what to do!"

I beg to differ, but instead of voicing that I stand, "If pain is something you desire then we can decide on something that is equally as safe. But let me be clear, you are *mine.* That means I *protect* what's mine, Little Bird. Even if that means protecting you, from you." I wait for a response, but she only pouts and moves towards the shower.

I follow behind her, waiting until she gets in before I undress. She watches wide eyed braiding her hair to the side as I take my shirt off and remove my pants, causing my dick to bob out. I smirk satisfied at her reaction before joining her.

The shower is more than spacious for two, but I press myself into her anyway, and smile as she fights back a quiet moan, still pouting, I'm sure. The water bounces from her skin onto mine as she stands facing the stream. I'd love to take her again, but this is supposed to be about aftercare.

So instead, I reach for her body wash and a washcloth, lathering it up. She turns to face me, "I'm surprised you don't have any tattoos." I pull her into me with my right arm and I begin washing her breast with my left, "I was never interested." She cranes her neck back and grabs the top of my arms as I scrub up higher.

"So, what are you interested in? Besides chasing girls out into the forest." I smirk, scrubbing over her shoulder then bring the washcloth back around to wipe down her stomach and down slightly between her thighs. "I like to cook," I say watching as she closes her eyes momentarily, "and I like the outdoors." She smiles at this, "Me too, I like being outside, in nature."

She allows me to continue to clean her. "So, what have you been doing all these years?" I ask curiously, wondering how she handled her family breaking up. I turn her around to wash her back. She sighs, "At first, nothing, I was so hurt and mad, I clung to my relationship with my mother because she was all I had left at the time. Following my mother's every command."

She pauses shaking, her head, "But when she met Thomas, he began to take all of her attention, I guess that's when I became rebellious. Getting my tattoos, even dropping out of college." I move to wring out the washcloth, then she begins to rise off.

"You don't like Thomas then?" I ask, eager to understand their relationship. She turns to face me, letting the water wash the soap away, "I do, it's just, I gave her every part of me, I allowed her to sculpt me, just to hear her praise. Until new men came into our lives, by the time she married Thomas, I became a shadow. A reminder of her past."

I grimace thinking back to when I overheard her mother in the church. We trade places and I reach for my body wash, "So why did you stay?" She wraps her arms over her breast, "I didn't. I tried to leave but only a week out on the street and that's when I realized I had nothing. I literally had no life outside of my mother. I didn't know the first thing about being on my own. Like how to write up a resume or how to be successful in a job interview." I want to tell her she won't ever have to worry about all of those things again, but I don't interrupt.

She scoffs, "I know how to sew, how to cook, and smile when I'm supposed to. It's like I learned nothing outside of serving others." Her parents did a number on her. I tilt my head smiling, "We have a lot of learning to do then, don't we Little Bird." She frowns in confusion as I finally rinse off.

I'm suddenly determined to learn everything about her, excited to unearth every desire, every tick. Blood rushes to my cock as I think about chasing her into the trees, what other kinks does she not know she has?

After our shower we dry off and make our way back to the bedroom. I smile, knowing this is where the real fun begins, I've put on a pair of boxers while she's thrown on a new pair of panties.

"Lay on the bed," I demand but she doesn't move. "I won't say it again Little Bird," I warn. "And if I don't?" She responds moving to clasp on a matching bra. I smile wickedly, "Then instead of a blissful orgasm, I can give you a torturous one." She rolls her eyes but makes her way over to bed. Satisfied, I move to grab a bottle of lotion and position myself at her feet.

Lifting one of her legs in my lap, I begin massaging the lotion into the soles of her foot, "How does that feel?" She watches me as she hums in satisfaction, "It feels good."

I take my time messaging her foot, before I move to the other. I make her take off the underwear set she just put on, so can do the same to the rest of her body. Taking special care of her thighs as I attempt to read her tattoo but then move to fondle her breast as I try to memorize every inch of her flesh.

By the time my hands move down her stomach she's shaking and taking deep quiet breaths. She whines, "August, *please*." Her voice sends shock waves to my cock. "You are so beautiful Little Bird," I say finally positioning myself upright between her legs, teasing her more by rubbing my cock against her pussy.

I want to fuck her senseless but still wanting to admire every inch of her. Her breasts are big and beautiful, her areolas are a darker shade than her brown skin, looking like tasty chocolate chips. I swoop down to kiss them and tease them with my teeth.

Hazel gifts me her moans, that has her trying to squeeze her legs together and her fingers moving to run in my hair. "Grab the bars above your head, baby." I instruct sitting up and she listens immediately, squeezing the bars of the bedframe and I make a note to reward her later for it.

"I want to see all of you," I say as if she isn't already on full display. I position myself at her entrance and tap against her clitoris before shoving deep inside her. She cries out, causing my cock to throb inside her walls. Pleasantly pleased at how wet she is, I praise her, "I think your pussy likes me more than you do." I slide out slowly before I set a pace while moving my hand to rub her clit, immediately she's moaning God's name which makes me see green.

"God's not here right now, not in this bedroom at least." I say pumping into her harder which causes her voice to rise and her legs to shake. She feels so fucking good on my cock, I moan with her. Then move to kiss her, taste her, and dominate her tongue. She moans into my mouth before calling out to him again.

How dare she call out to God when it's me making her shake. I move my right arm around her waist, still using my left to rub her clit. This position allows me to stroke harder and deeper, her moans turn into cries as her arms move from the bars to my chest to try and push me away from her, "August, no! It's too much!"

Her legs shake more violently as she's tethering at the edge. I grit out, "I don't think it's enough." I press my upper body into her hands drilling into her ruthlessly as pleasure from her voice coils down my spine. I feel her clench around me as tears brim her eyes. "August!" She begs, still pushing her hands against me.

The pleasure from her pussy and her voice pushing me closer to ecstasy. "That's right Little Bird, let me be your undoing," I groan into her ear. She begins to take deeper breaths, "It's too much!" She takes a long deep breath, squinting her eyes shut, "August!" Her cries flood my ears as her orgasm washes over her.

My cock feels like it's going to explode any second, "That's right baby, come all over me." As she continues to come down from the high, the idea of coming inside her, filling her womb with my seed, already has me groaning and taking slower strokes.

Hazel lifts to my ear, "Please come inside me, I need you too." Her words flow like music notes from heaven in my ears, sending me over a cliff, "Fuck!" Just as my cock starts to spurt out cum, I pull out stroking out most of it onto her stomach.

As I catch my breath, I look down at Hazel, who's slightly sitting up on her elbows and she's got a frown on her face. "You just came, twice tonight. Why are you frowning?" I ask, moving from on top of her, to sit beside her. She begins, "You pulled out." Hazel huffs continuing, "Is it because I'm not on birth-control?" I grin standing now that my breathing is normal, "No baby. You let go of the bars." I turn, leaving the room to get a towel for her.

8. Maxxie

This morning Rachel calls to let me know she'll be picking me up to go to the Diner for my unofficial interview and tour.

August left already for his morning run, so I'm focusing on getting ready. I'm dressing down today, choosing to wear black yoga pants and a loose purple t-shirt.

My lace front is still in good condition, and after brushing out my hair I settle for a neat low bun. I grab my cell phone and head to the kitchen and make slightly burnt toast and some coffee for Breakfast.

Soon I hear August opening up the sliding door and he grins as soon as his face meets mine, "Morning." The front of his shirt is soaked in sweat. He passes me and I take a sip of my coffee, "Good morning." I watch as he continues down the hall, soon returning to the kitchen shirtless.

The sweat on his body makes his skin glisten, my eyes travel to his v-line, stirring something hot in the pit of my stomach. August clears his throat, "Have you eaten breakfast?" He moves to grab my cup from me and takes a sip. "I had toast," I reply. He scoffs handing my cup back to me, "That's not breakfast. When are you supposed to be at the café?"

He's still standing in front of me, and I feel the heat radiating from his body. "Rachel told me we'd be there by 9:30 a.m." He nods, "Come with me." He turns around to head for the hallway again and I quickly set down my cup before following him.

August opens up the second bedroom door allowing me to walk in first. I thought this was simply a guest bedroom but to my surprise he's made the room a private office. There's a small window that faces the front of the house and a wide wooden and metal desk near the center of the room. A small bookshelf of classics sits on the right wall and two large black and white décor paintings hang on the left.

When he walks in, he goes straight to the black laptop sitting closed on the desk, "This is where I work during the day." My attention still on the paintings he calls me, "Come here Hazel." My head snaps at him and I cross my arms, "Why are you so demanding?"

He's already got the laptop open clicking away at something, but my feet are still in place. "Why are you hard of hearing?" He shoots back at me, his eyes not leaving the screen. "Ask nicely," I challenge.

This catches his attention and a dark grin spreads across his face, "That's one."

"One what?"

"That's one spanking I owe you, care to add to it?" He stands now moving towards me and my face widens in shock. A *spanking.* Does he think I'm a freaking child? "Thought so," he says reaching for my wrist, tugging me to the chair and pushing me down into it. "Now," he continues, "Let's work on that resume."

"My resume?" I say, finally focusing on the screen. There's an open word document with the title of *Hazel's Resume* and my basic information typed out. My insides fill with fuzziness and excitement. I look up at him, "Okay."

So, we spend the next ten minutes creating my first resume and even though Rachel already promised me a position at the diner, August prints it out for me to take anyway.

Rachel pulls into the driveway. "Hi Hazel!" She says as she gets out of the car to pop her trunk. I walk over to her with August right behind me. "Hi Rachel, what's this?" I ask as she lifts open the trunk hood.

"It's your wedding gifts, it's not a lot but I thought I'd bring them since I'm picking you up. August, do you mind taking these insides? We don't want to be late." He nods at her before turning to me, "I'll see you later, Hazel baby." He doesn't look too happy now that I'm actually leaving, but that's not my problem.

I hurry to the passenger seat and buckle in, more excitement coursing through me once August finally closes the trunk, taking the last of the gifts inside the house. Rachel puts the car in reverse. "Do you mind listening to some music?" she asks while flipping to turn on something random. It's catchy but she turns the volume down, only using it as background noise.

"So how do you like being back in town?" She asks as I can no longer see August's house. "It's okay. I'm surprised I didn't recognize more people at the food drive," I reply honestly. She smiles, "Yeah over the years a lot of the locals moved out and a bunch of new ones moved in. It's nice though, horribly quiet, but still nice."

"Quiet huh, well what do you guys do for fun?" I ask curiously. "Well, when Larson's not busy with the church, we like to drive to the next town over. They have so much more to do over there like mini golf, museums, and such beautiful duck parks," She replies happily. "Sounds like fun."

We get to the diner and the outside of the building looks old, but the inside is kept in shape. A mix of red, yellow, and blue coat the walls and the booths. This was definitely a 90's diner, I mean it's even got checker floors.

Maxxie is surprisingly an older man. I have to fix my face as he walks out behind the grill with sweat stains on the center of his off-white shirt. "Hazel! It's so nice to meet you!" His voice is loud and bumpy like there's a permanent vibrator in his neck. His hair is balding in the center. "It's nice to meet you too Maxxie," I say as I reach to shake his hand, but he pulls me into a hug.

"It's good to have you, I'm glad Rachel will finally have some help on the floor. I much prefer the grill," he says, smiling and I realize he hasn't let go of me yet. I step back and show him my resume, causing him to drop his arms.

He smiles down at it briefly, "Looks good, you're hired, but it is only part time. Rachel will show you the ropes. Holler if you've got any questions, I'll be back by the grill."

With that he walks off, and my smile drops as he does. Rachel steps in front of me, "I know he's handsy but don't let it bother you too much, and the tips make up for the pay." She winks at the last part then she pulls me along.

I spend all morning shadowing her well into the lunch hour. At first my nerves were getting the best of me but when Rachel stopped walking over to save me, I forced myself to watch closer and catch on faster.

When the clock suddenly hits 1p.m. Maxxie tells me I did good work and can leave for the day. Now I'm standing out front waiting for August to pick me up with Rachel on her lunch.

"I'm so happy August let you have this job. He was so upset about it at first, saying you didn't have to work and all, but well you know sometimes us ladies just need time away from our men," She giggles and I'm a little dumb founded. He *let* me have this job. "I'm glad too," I simply say out loud. I need to figure out a plan, as much as I feel butterflies around him or how good his dick is, a cage is still a cage.

August finally roles in, jumping out of the car to open my door. We wave bye to Rachel as I get in. "So, how was your first big day?" he asks. "Fine," I respond rolling my eyes. He makes a face but doesn't probe. We ride in silence as anger boils underneath my skin.

Wen we're back at the house, I quickly race in, not allowing August to get out another word before I make it into the bathroom. I lock the door and begin searching on my phone for the cheapest flight tickets I can find to anywhere but here.

I can pocket the money from the Diner, since August clearly doesn't want me working anyways. If I can save up enough to leave, then I'll be free. Pounding on the door pulls me from my consciousness, "Hazel, open the door."

I move to unlock and swing the door open spouting, "What do I need your permission to use the bathroom too!" I push past him into the living room, and he grabs my wrist, stopping me. Confusion and irritation cover his features, "What happened at the Diner?" I lean against the wall opposite of him yelling, "Nothing happened!"

I briefly put my head in my hand before looking back up at him, His hands are clenched, and he's breathing deeply. "You don't get to control me! I've dealt with that my entire life! You don't get to tell me what to do or even how to breathe! You don't *own* me!" I spit out my rage, and before I can take my next breath, he's on me, pushing me into the wall with one hand around my neck and the other digging into my hip.

I gasp expecting him to squeeze but he's only applying pressure. He moves to whisper in my ear, his lips barely grazing it, "Let me be perfectly clear Little Bird. You. Are. Mine." His hand on my hips squeezes into my skin, "I'll tell you what to do as I see fit. Where to kneel. When to eat."

He presses himself into me sliding his knee between my legs and heat shoots in between my thighs. He continues in a low voice, "and how to say thank you when I make you come." I hiss, "Never." His right hand around my neck squeezes ever so slightly, "Oh, you will Little Bird."

His hand on my hip moves down to my stomach diving quickly under the fabric of my yoga pants. I gasp at the contact of his skin. "You'll beg me to make you come," His fingers find the bulb of my clit. I try to squeeze my thighs together, but he has me pinned.

"Do you want to come right now, Little Bird?" He asks and I hold my breath as his fingers dip further down into my treacherous pussy. The feeling causing me to moan. He grins, his breath against my neck, "Or shall I spank that bratty ass of yours?" My walls clench around his fingers involuntarily at his words.

But then I move to push him off of me and he lets me, taking a step back into the wall behind him. I slap him across the face, still drumming with adrenaline. He doesn't move for a second let the sting seep in before he says, "That's two." My eyes widen, and I grab my hand, no fucking way he's still counting. "You can sleep in the living room tonight," I say, mimicking harshness.

He smiles, biting back, "Is our honeymoon phase over already?" I don't respond waiting for his next move. He leaves though, walking into his office and shutting the door behind him. I run back into the bathroom desperate to wipe my wetness away. Reminding myself a cage is still a cage, even if it's hot and dangerous.

9. Bestfriends are just like siblings; Annoying

AUGUST

After shutting my office door, I immediately grip my throbbing cock trying to take a deep breath. I didn't think having such a bratty wife would be a turn on, but fuck, I think she's like a little pain with her pleasure. I'll have to further test that theory. I move to sit in my office chair.

My cock pulsing again as I remember her body reacting to my words. I think I enjoy pressing her buttons as well. Watching as anger overcame her features, how it breaks her character, that mask she wears out in public like everything is fine.

It's hot knowing there's a feisty woman beneath it and now I'm glad she's not completely submissive. There's so much to explore there. My cock leaks precum and I groan giving into the fantasy of all the possibilities with my Little Bird.

The sound of crunching leaves fill my ears as Hazel, and I walk in silence. We're in the heart of town today, in need of a few things. We walk into a local hardware store, Hazel's dresser came but they forgot to ship the screws. My phone pings for the second time in 5 minutes. She makes a face but doesn't say anything. I know she's wondering why I won't answer it. We leave as quickly as we came.

I hold open the door to the next place on the list, Pinky's Salon. I think Hazel's hair looks fine, but she insists it needs to be touched up. We walk up to the counter where the DJ from our wedding sits writing away. Hazel immediately begins taking off her coat, exposing that beautiful dark purple dress that shows off her curves.

She speaks, handing it to me, "Hi Justin!" He snaps up at the sound of her voice, "Hi Hazel." He stands moving closer to us, to *her*, "What a pleasure seeing you again, what can I help you with?" His eyes wander briefly down her body, making me step closer to her. Clearing my voice I say, "She needs her hair done, we don't have an appointment. Can you squeeze her in?" Only now does he look at me, "Of course we can."

He turns back to her, "Moms should be finish-ing up in ten minutes, but maybe I can help you?" My blood boils at the thought of him touching her. She smiles at him, "Oh, that won't be necessary, we're in no rush. Thanks Justin!" Hazel begins to move to a couple of waiting chairs and I walk behind her blocking his view.

We sit and my phone pings again. There are only a few other people in the room, but the buzz of conversation dulls it out. She asks, "Have you been here before?" I pull out my phone, checking the time before I respond, "I have not."

She seems to have expected that answer and says, "This was one of my safe spaces back then, Cathy is my safe space." I nod taking in the information. It's no secret we weren't in the same crowds back in high school.

My phone pings again and she takes a deep breath, I can feel the irritation rubbing off of her but what she doesn't know is, It's Daniel and Caleb bothering me about her. It's only been a little over a week since our wedding and I'm not ready for them to meet her yet.

Hazel's gaze lifts as an elderly woman comes into view, "Hazel, What a surprise!" She heads over to us, and Hazel and I stand. I recognize her, she used to come to church all the time before the shit with our parents, and I saw her talking to Hazel at the after party.

"Hi Cathy!" Hazel's voice sounds like music in the room as people glance over. I look up to Justin watching the interaction which makes me move to rest my left hand on her lower back. Cathy says, "I'm surprised to see you so soon. Have you been drinking the fertility blend I made you?" My eyebrows knit in confusion as I feel Hazel stiffen beside me, but she doesn't show her discomfort as she laughs looking up at me, "Not yet."

"We look forward to drinking it," I don't know why I say it but it's already in the air and I feel Hazel burning holes into me with her eyes. Cathy briefly smiles at me before she says, "Excellent! Well then, let's touch up your lace and see what else we can do." Without another word she grabs Hazel's hand tugging her into a beauty chair five feet away from me. I sit back down as my phone pings again, and I curse as I pull it out quickly. It reads:

Daniel: Come on, we'll run into her eventually, might as well be there before we sink our claws into her.

I know he's teasing but I take a deep breath anyway. The image of him and Caleb touching her fills my head, and I begin to see red. To make it worse, he starts to call. I ignore the first two rings and Cathy speaks, "Aren't you going to get that?" She hasn't turned her face from Hazel. I fake a laugh, "It's nothing." Still focusing on Hazel's hair she responds, "Seems like *nothing* really wants to talk to you." The ringing stops and I silence my phone.

About an hour has passed when Hazel finally stands from the chair. Her hair now has fresh loose curls, still looking as beautiful as ever. I'm not sure what else Cathy did to her hair, but she seems pleased. I head back to the counter to pay the total as Hazel finishes saying goodbye.

Justin and I finish the transaction in silence until Hazel's at my side. "Oh, Hazel, here, take my number." He moves, handing her a square card and my eyes widen. He continues, "In case you need a DJ for another party." Before she can reach up, I swipe it from him, "Thanks, will do." I turn towards the door as I hear Hazel tell him goodbye.

As soon as we're outside I take a deep breath, trying to remain calm because we're still in public, "That's three." I turn to walk back to the car tugging her behind me. She whispers, frustration clear in her voice, "*Three!* But I didn't do anything!"

I don't respond until we're back into the car and away from watching eyes, "He was giving you his number, right in front of me." I grip the steering out of frustration.

She fights back though, "For professional use! Besides I'm not the one hiding anything *Mr. doesn't want to answer his phone around his wife!* You think I haven't noticed? Don't think for one second that I'll play along as your little housewife while you go sticking your dick in other people! If you didn't want to be monogamous, you shouldn't have married me!" She fumes out the last of her fury and I start to laugh in relief.

I haven't cared about being monogamous before, and it's only now that I'm realizing that's exactly what I want with her. I look at her briefly and of course she's looking at me wide eyed.

With my eyes back on the road I exhale, "I'm not cheating on you Hazel. It's my friends; they want to meet you." I glance back over at her, and her features soften, "I'm just not ready to share you yet."

Her angry disappears as she speaks, "Well lucky for you, you don't have to share me, not in that sense anyway, but I want the same from you, August. Promise me there's nobody else." I feel relief washing over me as I say, "I promise Little Bird."

We arrive in front of Larson's and Rachel's place. Out-front in the cold, I see Rachel place what looks like a small shoe box into the soil before quickly planting a marigold on top of it. I get an queasy feeling and my heart sinks a little. Once she sees us approaching, she smiles standing to dust her gloves, "Hey guys, Larson's in the kitchen. Let me finish up out here and I'll be in soon."

I nod, passing her and guiding Hazel into the house. Larson is nothing like our father when it comes to being luxurious. Their house is an old 80's family home with rustic wood and creaking steps to the second floor. I know it's a three bed two bathroom, and while I think they should renovate it, he swears the creaks and peeling paint gives the house character.

Finding him in the kitchen at the dinner table, he immediately greets us, "Glad you guys made it! It's good to see you again Hazel." He lifts his beer and continues, "Rachel made some pesto chicken sliders for lunch if you want to grab a bite."

Hazel smiles, "Sounds good." She glances up at me before making her way further into the kitchen. I take a seat with Larson, "What's this?" I look at the papers in front of him as he responds, "Some letters and bills from the church, it seems you and Hazel have sparked the interest of the town and the church."

He holds up a letter along with a check, "This donation came the next day, after your wedding and this one," He holds up another, "Came the Sunday evening after the service that you and Hazel attended. I'm not sure I believe this, but I think dad's plan is working."

I sigh running my hands through my hair remembering that Sunday. There were more people than the week before even though it's not what it used to be. Even at the food drive, more people showed up than normal. "It's progress," I finally respond. I'm happy they believe it's working but I hope dad doesn't start trying to press me into every single event. There's a reason Larson is taking over the Pastor role when he steps down.

Rachel comes back inside quickly pouring us all a glass of water as Hazel brings two plates from the kitchen and sets one in front of me. I'm a little surprised she was thinking about me, "Thank you." She sits down beside me, turning her attention to Rachel who's joined us at the table, "How long have you been gardening for?" She takes a bite of her slider while Rachel responds, "Longer than I'd like to admit."

She sighs, setting down her glass, "but it brings me peace." Larson shifts uncomfortably in his chair, "How do you like being back in town Hazel? It seems the town enjoys your presence." She finishes chewing before responding and laughs, "Everyone keeps asking me that." I move to rest my hand in her lap. She doesn't seem uncomfortable but still.

Larson responds, "Hey, I get it, maybe your presence will bless us in more ways than one." I look at him, what the Hell is he getting at? He looks briefly at Rachel but speaks under his breath, "Unlike *others*, maybe you'll bear more fruitful." The fuck? "Larson don't be a dick," I immediately snap at him, but he stands from the table dismissing himself.

I turn to Rachel, "I'm sorry my brothers an ass, Rachel." She shakes her head dismissively, "It's fine. He's just losing his faith." She stands. Rushing to make her feel better I say, "Look there's this herbalist I know, they make this great Fertility blend, I'll bring it next time we see you." I know I fibbed a little, but I know she won't accept it if she knows it's ours. She weakly smiles, "Thank you. You guys should leave, I need to rest."

We leave without another word. The light in this sky is dim as the sun begins to set. It's not until we reach the car, Hazel asks, "How long have they been struggling with fertility?"

I sigh as I open her car door and she gets in, "Since they started trying." I shut the door behind her getting in myself. Fishing for my keys and starting the car I continue, "Sorry about the tea blend, I was just being nice." She shrugs looking out the car window as we take off, "It's fine, it's not like we were going to use it anyway." I frown, not sure why her words sting but it does, "Yeah."

My phone pings again and this switches her whole mood, "For the love of God if you don't respond back to them I will."

"Fine," I reply. She isn't interested in three-somes, so hopefully they don't tempt her, "We'll go meet them. Not today though, I've shared you with enough people today." She rolls her eyes at this but doesn't respond.

Instead, she lets me drive with my hand on her thigh into comfortable silence. I'm not sure if she's noticed we're not heading home by now. Regardless she sits content watching the sun fade beneath the horizon.

We've been driving for almost thirty minutes now, and she hasn't questioned where we're going until we pull into the parking lot of an abandoned church. "What is this?" She sits up asking as I drive slowly, parking close to the main doors.

The moonlight is the only source of light here. The trees cover most of the lot and some of the church windows are either broken or boarded up, "This is where I come to clear my head." I get out of the car and the breeze sends chills throughout my body.

Hazel doesn't wait for me to open her door as I walk around the car to meet her. "The church back home is tainted in a weird way. Here, it's untouched." She loops her hand in my arm saying, "Well I can see that." I guide her to the side of the building where I know the side door is unlocked.

We walk inside, and head straight to the altar where I know I've hidden a lighter. Once I discovered this place, I brought a dozen candles and changed the locks, just to make it my own. She watches me as I light every single one. The candles give the room a warm dim light, I sign in satisfaction and move to sit in the first row.

Still standing by the altar Hazel says, "This feels romantic." She crosses her arms probably from the cold. I grin, "Does it?" She doesn't respond, looking more around the room. "When the shit with our parents happened, I left home dog set on leaving my family and this life. On the way I stumbled upon this place, and I guess I just never left," I say, feeling a pain in my chest at the memory of our childhood.

Hazel finally walks over to me, but instead of sitting beside me, she stops in between my legs. She wraps her arms around my shoulders and her fingers drift to the back of my hair. My cock pulses from the contact, but I find it oddly comforting.

"I'm glad you had somewhere to escape," she says quietly.

I pull her closer to me, wrapping my arms around her waist. I move, resting the left side of my face on her stomach, closing my eyes, finding contentment within her. For a moment she runs her hands through my hair before saying, "You know, you're kind of cute when you're not so bossy." Reluctantly I pull myself away from her to look up at her, "Is that so?"

She smiles, still holding me and I can't help but notice how the moonlight and dim room makes her look angel-like. Her plump lips, pink in the center that darkens on the outer side. Even the width of her nose looks sculpted to perfection, eyes are round and beautifully brown. She steps away, breaking my trance, "Stop staring at me like that."

I stand immediately following her to the empty altar at the front of the room, "Now look who's being bossy?" She rolls her eyes but smiles as she leans against it for support, "Mr. Forkhill I doubt that even God himself could boss you around." I move closer to her, wrapping my arms around her waist. Her eyes widen and her smile fades, whispering, "August, *please.*"

I don't respond. Wondering if she has anything else to say but nothing else falls from her lips. So, I step back nodding to the altar she's leaning on, "Sit." She looks behind herself at the wooden table saying, "And if I don't?" Warmth spreads through me as she challenges, "I can always make you." A smile dares to creep upon her lips, "What if I say no?" My cock pulse as her voice fuels me, "We both know that's not how you say no."

I wait as she leans further against it but doesn't move to sit. Still, she says nothing lust filling in her eyes. I grin, pouncing on her. I move to lift her onto it, sitting her down with a loud plop and she giggles wrapping her arms around my neck, "It's cold."

"Too bad," I respond, pushing up her dress. She gasps again as my fingers rub against her stockings, blocking her skin from mine. I run my right hand slowly up her thigh feeling every goosebump in place. Finally, I cup her pussy through the weak fabric earning myself a moan from her lips. I could have her here so easily, "I want to taste you Little Bird."

Before she can respond, I rip the fabric between her legs, exposing her more to the cold. She gasps as she watches me. I look down at her parted lips as I move her panties to the side. My fingers are cold against her skin, but her pussy feels hot against my hand.

"You don't like to ask, but your pussy knows exactly what she wants," I speak filth into the air before moving to kiss her. I quickly stick two fingers inside her, and she jolts underneath me, moaning into my mouth. Blood rushes to my already hardening cock as I feel the heat of her around my fingers. She may be sitting on this altar, but she is no offering. In this moment I feel the need to show God just how much she belongs to me.

10. Always pray over your meals

It's been eleven days since we've been married, and Halloween is tomorrow night. August goes back to work this morning which is perfectly fine considering he's just in the other room.

I'm dressed casually with dark green yoga pants, long black socks that come close to my thighs, and a nude long-sleeve sweater while on the phone with Rachel sitting mindlessly in the living room.

"Larson's going fishing with John today, not sure if you had any plans but I could use the company," Rachel says, sounding happier today. Emotions squeeze at my heart as I remember the last time I was over there, "Of course I'd love to come by Rachel." It'll be nice to be away from August for a while, plus I can bring that fertility blend.

"Okay, great, you can help me organize some of the youth's costumes for tomorrow and who knows, maybe even pick one out for me." I move looking towards August office door, before asking, "You're dressing up?"

She replies laughing, "Well I volunteered to take out some of the kids from our church youth group, so yes, I would like to. Aren't you?" I only trust a handful of places, for plus size clothes and most of them are online, and it's way too late to order anything for it to be here by tomorrow, "Uh I don't know."

"Why not? I'm sure we can find you something." She presses. "We'll see," I reply, wanting to drop the discussion. "Okay. I'll see you when you get here." We hang up and I get up walking down the hall.

I knock before walking into August's office. He's sitting through a video call, and I don't speak at first drinking in the sight of him dressed in a full grey suit, with a plaid tie and everything.

It's moments like this, or when he's fucking me senseless that I forget our marriage isn't normal and he's annoyingly controlling. "Yes, Hazel baby?" He says using the nickname he calls me in front of people, which means his mic isn't muted. I whisper, "Rachel wants me to come over." I can hear a female's voice and for some reason it rubs me wrong.

"You can take the car, be back by noon, we're supposed to be meeting the guys later." He says and I sigh. So demanding. I walk more into the room because how do I tell him, driving is just another thing I didn't learn, another way my mother kept her claws on me.

Seeing the look on my face, he interrupts the women speaking, "Sounds good so far, let's take a break and we'll discuss it more later." In a few seconds he ends the call, relaxing a little. "I don't know how to drive," I finally say embarrassingly.

He stares at me a moment before standing up and saying, "Come on, we'll add it to the bucket list." I frown as he grabs his keys and other things from his desk, "I don't have a bucket list." He moves towards me grabbing my wrist, "We're making it up as we go."

Next thing I know he's hauling my ass into the driver's seat in an empty parking lot. "August no! I just want to go to Rachel's!" I yell as he shuts the driver door in my face. I huff watching him run over to the passenger side.

It's not that I don't want to learn, but this is a nice car, and I don't want to crash it. That and I really do just want to go to Rachel's house. He gets in, shuttling his door, "Stop being a brat, I just showed you some basic maneuvers, once you've done that, I'll take you to Rachel's."

"That could literally take all day," I whine, "What about your job! You said you were going on a break; I don't want you getting in trouble." He runs his fingers through his hair, clearly getting irritated with me, "Vanessa will have no problem sending in an email what she was saying in the video call. You are more important, Little Bird. I need you to be able to do this in case I can't be there."

His words shouldn't be affecting me the way that they are, there's no reason him telling me I'm important turns my fuse to butter, melting in the base of my stomach. "Okay fine," I huff smacking both my hands onto the steering wheel.

He laughs reaching over me to buckle my seat belt, then his own. "Put your foot on the break before you start the car." I move, doing as he says and when the car roars to life he continues, "Now put the gear in drive and slowly take your foot off the break. We're doing the basics just a straight shot across the lot."

Anxiety blooms in my chest as I put the car in drive, it begins to move as I slowly lift my foot off the petal. "Oh shit," I say under my breath squeezing the wheel tighter. "Relax Little Bird, you've got it, no need to turn the wheel but I want you to give it a little gas, lightly press the gas pedal with the top of your foot."

His praise gives me courage as I do as he says, and the car begins to move faster. Excitement begins to mix with my anxiety as we cross half of the lot. "That's it, now ease off the gas and come to a slow by easing your foot back onto the brake pedal."

I don't hesitate to lift my foot and move it successfully, bringing the car to a slow and complete stop. I put the car in park as I burst with excitement, "Oh my God! I did it!" I unbuckle my seat belt, my excitement mixing with lust as I look over at a grinning August.

"Yes, you did. Now, get in the back seat."

I open my door quickly getting in the backseat, excitement still coursing through me as I ask, "Why?" He pulls up the front passenger seat before getting out and joining me in the back, "Wouldn't you like a reward?" My pussy pulses at his words but before he can do anything else I move to kneel in the new space between his legs behind the passenger seat.

It's tight but not uncomfortable. His windows aren't tinted but I don't care, I'm too excited. "Take your cock out," I demand. "You don't want a reward?" He smirks, while still not moving. Eagerness makes me impatient, so I move to unbuckle his pants for him, "This is a reward."

He allows me to undo his belt and zipper and his cock pops out already hardening. He's cut and his head's a darkish pink, prettier than it should be. I grab him with my hands first, feeling his girth makes my mouth water.

He pulls my hair back as I move to lick his tip and he hisses. Tasting the saltiness of precum, I swirl my tongue around his head, and I feel him growing in my hands.

He moans again as I swoop down, taking all of him in my mouth. He's thick and hard and now my pussy wants him. I ignore my body as I begin sucking on his cock. "Fuck yes," he grits out under his breath, his voice clouding me in pillows of lust.

My head bobs as I feel drool sliding from the corners of my mouth. "That's right baby, be a good girl and take all of me." I hum with his cock still I'm my mouth, feeling myself getting wet from his voice. He takes over, holding my head in place as I move my left hand to touch myself through my yoga pants. "Such a good girl," He purrs as he fucks my face.

Briefly I think about being able to have him, however I want, every single day, but I push the thought in the back of my head and continue to enjoy this experience. Soon his pace weakens as his cum floods into my mouth.

He moans profanities as he slows, coming down from the high. He tastes bittersweet as I let him pump out every ounce. Finally, he pulls out sitting back and I swallow his load. He grins down at me before moving to kiss me passionately, I'm sure he can taste himself on me as his tongue dances with mine. My pussy is still dripping wet, but we're in public and anyone could have seen, "Let's get to Rachel's."

We ride in comfortable silence on the way over and I hear him murmur something about the tint. When we arrive, Rachel's waiting out front. I grab the jar of tea and August says, "I'll be back in a little while." He reaches for my left hand as I hold the jar in my right and brings it to hips lips, placing a simple gentle kiss, "Be good Little Bird." I roll my eyes as he lets go and I move to open the door. "No promises," I wink getting out the car.

"You made it!" Rachel says as I approach her. "Yeah," I say as heat rushes to my face as if she knew what we were doing. "Here, it's not much but I hope it helps," I say handing her the jar of herbal fertility tea blend. "Thank you!" she says graciously.

"Let's go test it out!" She smiles, turning to head for the house and I follow her. We walk past the flowers she was planting the other day, and I remember the little box underneath. That's when I realize there are four of them, four identical flowers. My heart aches as I have no doubt there are similar boxes under the other three, and they're definitely not empty.

We enter her home which looks the same as last time, the energy feels lighter though. "How long have you and Larson been together?" I ask, but immediately regret it, unsure if she wants to talk about him. I take a seat at the kitchen table as she moves to grab a kettle. "Oh, we've been together for six years now, we got married after our first three months together."

"Wow," I respond. That's commitment. "Yes, my mother thought I was crazy too," she laughs, filling the kettle with water and placing it on the stove. "You're not crazy," I say, trying to amend the offense. "Yes, well…" she trails off as she joins me at the table.

"You don't regret it? I mean do you ever think you're missing out on what's out there?" I say gesturing to the world around us. I probably shouldn't be asking, but I'm curious.

She smiles, "You only miss out on things when you're looking elsewhere. I mean sure, there were moments of doubt caused by fear, but love is like a garden, you have to tend to it, for it to grow."

A few minutes later and the kettle begins to whistle, Rachel beams, "The water's ready!" I watch, contemplating her words as she moves to scoop a spoonful of the tea blend into a filter before pouring the hot water over it. "It smells good," I say as the smell of raspberries, peppermint, and ginger fill the air.

She quickly pours two cups, bringing them to the table, "Hopefully it works." She hands me a white coffee cup before we both move to sip it at the same time. "Mmm," she moans. The ginger is overpowering as the tea runs into my mouth and down my throat. I take another sip though, as the warmth is welcoming, "It's strong, but it tastes good."

After we finish the tea, we move to her living room, and she pulls out a big black bag of childlike costumes, "I have a list of names, so we just have to sort the costumes to the names. Hopefully, we have enough for everyone." She moves to grab the list setting it on the floor between us. Then she dumps the clothes out and we begin sorting. We sit in comfortable silence as we focus on the task at hand.

After everything is sorted and organized, we stand and my legs feel all crampy, August should be pulling up any minute, "Thanks for having me over." She stands dusting off her hands asking, "So are you still not wanting to dress up?" I smile, "It's not that I don't want to, I just don't have something to wear." Rolling her eyes she says, "Don't be silly."

Then she immediately rummages through the left-over costumes picking up a black headband of cat ears, "Here, hold on." She hands it to me then quickly heads out of sight. I laugh internally before she comes back with a small black paint bottle, "Paint on the nose and whiskers, and you can be a cat for Halloween." I smile and laugh, "Thanks Rachel."

We hear a car honk from out front, "That must be August." I point to the door. She smiles, "Of course, let me walk you out." Rachel walks with me all the way to August's car before saying, "Thank you again for the tea, until next time." I wave as I open the car door, "Bye Rachel."

August waits until I've closed the door and Rachels walking back to the house to ask, "Did you have fun?" I place the cat ears and paint in my lap as I move to put my seatbelt on, "Yeah I guess I did." August reaches behind the back passenger seat, "I got you something." He sets it in my lap and moves to start the car, "We're meeting the guys at a bar, I want you to wear it there."

The car's gears into motion as I move to open the bag, my face heats as I pull out a pink small remote-control vibrator, "August!" I stare in disbelief as he grins, "Don't worry it's out of town so you don't need to worry about watching eyes."

Still holding the packaged egg shaped toy in my hand, he continues, "Open it and put it in."

I look at him wild-eyed, "You want me to wear this, in front of your friends?" He laughs, "No one will know. Now put it on, or I'll pull over and help you." I frown although the tiniest bit of excitement runs through my veins as I begin to open it. First, I open the controller and set it in the middle cup holder. August swipes it, saying, "I'll take that, thank you."

I roll my eyes as I get the actual vibrator out. It's silicone material and it's soft. August keeps his eyes on the road as he says, "Get it wet." This shouldn't be turning me on the way it is as I move the toy up to my lips slowly sticking out my tongue licking all around and briefly submerging it in my mouth. I hear August curse, stealing glances at me before I move to pull down my yoga pants. I pull my black lace aside and slowly begin to push it in.

After fully inserting it inside me, I pull my yoga pants back up and readjust to the feeling. August is trying to hide a smirk, and I say sarcastically, "Happy now." He bites his bottom lip, "Very. Should we test it?" I take a deep breath of anticipation not answering him and he leaves his left hand on the steering wheel as he clicks the control in his right hand.

The vibrator jolts to life and I gasp feeling the overwhelming sensation inside me, "Oh fuck." I breath out clenching around it. "Do you like that Little Bird?" he asks, as lust fills his voice. "August," I say focusing on the pleasure. Just as quickly he turns it off saying, "I think you'll do just fine."

11. Punishment? You mean funishment!

I sit watching life pass by in the window, I believe we're just in the next town over as the drive isn't too long. August is wearing casual jeans and a grey top, but I wish we had stopped at the house. I'm literally in a sweater and yoga pants and this is a bar for crying out loud.

"Comfortable?" August asks with a smirk as he holds open the door to the establishment. "Mhm," I hum, the vibrator definitely giving me an edge as I walk.

He guides me inside and the bars in full swing. There are a few wooden tables and chairs off to the side as well as a pool table and a dart game. The actual bar is straight ahead with two busy bartenders. Bartender by T-pain plays in the background, it's clearly a hole in the wall place and I relax a little knowing no one from town could possibly be here.

"August!" two guys yell his name from our left side. August tenses beside me guiding us over to them. We sit across from them as he says, "Hazel baby, this is Daniel and Caleb my best friends." I wave nervously at them, "Hi."

I'm sitting directly across from Daniel as he speaks, "Congratulations! It's great to finally meet you!" He's got reddish hair and a horribly boyish grin. I feel August left hand slide down my lower back. Caleb smiles darkly at the both of us, "So what do you care to drink? Blowjobs anyone?"

I answer before August can speak for me, "Yes please!" I feel August staring holes into the side of my face as Caleb laughs brushing back his arm length locks, "Shots are on me!" He stands leaving to the bar.

I finally turn to August, giving him an innocent smile, "Relax August, I can handle myself." Daniel laughs, grabbing our attention, "Oh, she seems feisty!" He taps the table in excitement. August smirks, "You have no idea." I see his right-hand slip into his pocket, and I tense, *oh shit*. I sit up more, moving my right hand to rest on his left thigh, "How come I didn't see you guys at the wedding?"

Daniel smiles focusing on me, "Oh we were there, and at the after party too. August must have forgotten about us." He makes a face, fake pouting. August replies too quickly, "Stop being dramatic and excuse me for being eager to spend time with my *wife*." Daniel holds his hands up in defense, "Whatever man."

Caleb comes back. holding four shots in his hands, "First shot is for the lady!" He sets them down and immediately hands one to me. "Thank you." I say and we down them throwing our heads back. The warmth after the cold makes me relax more. "Woo!" Daniel yells, shaking his head dramatically as he slams down his shot glass.

I smile to myself he seems like such a character, "So, how did you guys meet August?" Daniel laughs responding, "We were next-door neighbors as kids. August was already up to no good when we started hanging out."

I laugh feeling August relax beside me. August responds, "Yeah well you weren't to good at keeping us out of shit either." I don't see why August was so pressed about me meeting them. He seems totally in his element around them. "Did you guys go to school together?" I ask, not remembering either of their faces from our childhood.

Caleb turns to me, answering, "I was home-schooled, but Daniel and August did." He swirls his finger on the rim of the empty glass. Daniel chimes in, "Yeah, August and I were inseparable back then." He bats his eyes, and August grunts, "You mean you followed me around like a sick puppy all damn day."

They laugh, and Caleb says, "Speaking of pets, thank you again for giving me mine. She's so *entertaining.*" I frown looking at August, "A pet? You gave him a puppy?" Suddenly, Daniel burst out laughing next to me. "No," August responds simply.

I wait for him to elaborate, confused, but he doesn't. "Let's play a game," August says while standing. This catches Daniel and Calebs attention. He nods towards the pool table, "You guys go set up the pool table, Hazel and I will be right there." I swear I see disappointment flash across their faces, but they stand heading over to the pool table.

Once they leave August moves to sit across from me and I ask, "So are you going to tell me why you gifted your friend a puppy or will I have to ask him?" Something flashes in his eyes, but he says, "Let's see if that toy still works."

Suddenly, the vibrator comes to life inside me and I squeeze my thighs together and try to fight back a moan. God dammit, why is it so strong? I close my eyes, putting my hand on the table trying my hardest to concentrate on not rubbing against the pleasure. He speaks lowly, "Look at you, trying so hard. Should I up the speed?" I breath out all too quickly, "Please don't." He grins before stopping the vibrator, and I relax, taking a breath.

He speaks quietly, "I've already told you Kim was my sub. Whatever partner she has now is no of my concern." *Kim?* Is that what he means? "So, he's dating your ex?" I say still gaining my composure, and unsure how that correlates with puppies. He simply nods. As a girl's girl, that seems so messed up, "That doesn't bother you?" He sighs, "I wasn't monogamous prior to our relationship, Little Bird."

His words shouldn't rile me the way they do. Jealousy dances on my tongue as I wonder about the girls before me, the girls who know what he feels like inside of them. Irritated, I say, "I need a drink." I move to stand, and he hands me his card, "Put it on my card. I'll be over at the pool table with the boys." I snatch his card walking away from him and towards the bar.

The bartenders are pretty busy as a dozen people try to get drinks all at once. I don't bother shoving past them. There are too many bodies, it'll just be an uncomfortable experience.

So, I wait but after a minute or two, I curse under my breath, my irritation rising. I feel watching eyes as I try to move closer in. "Need help?" A light, unfamiliar voice calls beside me. I turn to see a handsome man with a drink already in his hand. "Um, no I've got it," I turn anyway, clearly ending the conversation. He speaks again, "Are you sure? I'm a regular here, I can get closer a lot faster." I step back crossing my arms, "Alright then, get me a drink."

He smirks moving past me. I finally look over to the pool table. They seem to be playing a game, but August is watching me with dark eyes. I smirk and within two minutes, Mr. random is back, handing me a drink and I get the wild urge to make August jealous.

I reach for the glass out of his hands, but use my other to lightly touch his chest, "Thank you." I barely push out the word before that damn vibrator is buttering up my insides. I nearly drop the glass, suddenly gripping it tight as if my life depended on it. I bite my lip, trying to fight the urge to squat to control the pleasure. The guy is now looking at me concerned, "Are you okay?" I nod, a flush of warmth flows to my cheeks, full of embarrassment at the thought of the guy in front me hearing the toy. Fuck me. I nod in response, "Here, you keep this." I hand the drink back to him. I take a breath clenching around the toy but that only makes it more pleasurable. Immediately I look for the bathroom, then rush to it, biting my lip to keep from embarrassing myself.

As soon as I walk through the doors it cuts off and I take another deep breath rushing to the sink. I place his card in my bra and rub my legs together feeling uncomfortably wet. I look around briefly to see that I'm alone, so I move to wash my hands to calm myself down. As soon as I turn on the water the door opens and my eyes widen as August walks in too calmly, locking the door behind him. Oh, I am so fucked.

"Hi Little Bird."

I don't move watching him in the mirror as he briefly looks down at the bathroom stalls then back to me. He moves, walking down the stalls slowly pushing open every single door. Fear and excitement bloom in my chest as I continue to watch him in the mirror, "Tell me does that ring on your finger signify anything?" I don't respond as adrenaline erupts in my body.

He finishes checking the last stall and questions, "No?" The dark edge to his voice spreads heat between my thighs. He finally walks towards me, "Maybe I'll need to put a collar on you instead." My eyes widen as his words, and he reaches me.

Wrapping his left hand around my neck and his right around my body, pulling me into him. I try to turn and face him, but he pushes me into the sink, the left side of my face and my hands land on the mirror to support myself.

"This pussy belongs to *me*, baby." He whispers into my right ear as I feel his right hand run down the front of my stomach. I respond the only way I know how, "Prove it then." I see a grin spread on his face, and he moves to pull down my yoga pants, "What's your safe word Little Bird." He moves his left hand pressing it into the middle of my back as his right-hand rubs over my ass. "Cupcakes," I whisper as the fabric of my panties follow my yoga pants, and I feel my heartbeat thumbing in my ears.

He moves to turn on the vibrator and I gasp for air as pleasure floods through me. Suddenly, I hear the sound before I feel the sting of him smacking my ass, "Owe!" I cry out but he holds me in place rubbing where he's inflicted the pain. "Shh Little Bird," he says before repeating the process a second time. I hiss closing my eyes as the pleasure mixes with pain. I'm so wet, I fear my vibrator will slip out.

He rub's the area again and by the third strike, I feel an orgasm building in the pit of my stomach. "August," I whine, and he rubs the area once more before bending down to kiss over the now sensitive skin. I open my eyes as he moves to turn off the vibrator, and as I'm still pinned against the mirror, he pulls out the pink toy saying, "open your mouth."

My eyes widen and he smirks, continuing, "Don't want anyone thinking you're in danger." Reluctantly I open my mouth, and he puts the toy inside. I can taste my juices and it's not uncomfortably big, but I definitely can't say anything. My hands are free so I could take it out if I really wanted to.

"Such a naughty little girl," He whispers against me before pulling out his cock and rubbing it against my pussy, "fuck, Little Bird, look how wet you are." His length feels so promising, I shiver with desire.

He speaks lowly, "To be clear Little Bird, this is not for your pleasure, this is me claiming what's mine. I am going to fuck you here for as long as I please. Then I'm going to come inside you, marking everything that belongs to me. Only after will you walk out of here with my cum dripping from your pussy." My insides turn at his promises, and I moan.

He grips my hips sliding inside me with ease, my eyes flutter from pleasure. He begins moving in and out of me, I moan what little I can. He speeds up though, pounding into me relentlessly, the sound of his skin clapping against mine floods my ears.

My pussy throbs with need as his grip on my hips tighten. "You have a beautiful fat ass, baby," I hear him moan, and I want to touch myself, I start to move my hand, but he pushes into me further, "Don't you dare, when I'm ready to let you come,

I will." I swear water brims my eyes as the pleasure is becoming unbearable, I whine.

He moves to take the vibrator out of my mouth as he says, "Who do you belong to, Little Bird? Say the right answer, and maybe I'll let you come." I breath out as soon as it's gone moaning into the air, "You August, I belong to you!" He spanks me lightly gritting out, "I don't believe you!" and he's right, he has no right to believe me it's not like I've made it easy. I cry out, "Fuck August!" I continue, begging, "I want to come so bad, *please* make me come!"

With that he pulls out of me, quickly turning me around and pushing back inside me, I moan wrapping my arms around him using the sink to hold up one of my legs. He moves to kiss me as one of his hands snakes down to rub my clit.

I feel so lost in the clouds as his tongue dances with mine, my orgasm nearing as I moan into his mouth. The pleasure of his cock inside me and his hands stroking my clit become overwhelmingly pleasurable, "Come for me Little Bird."

In a few seconds I do, I come hard and loud, he tries to muffle my voice with kisses before his pace changes to deep strokes. "Please come inside me," I beg still high from the experience. Soon he's moaning profanities as his cock pulses inside me and the warmth of his cum feels oddly pleasurable.

His pace slows and he pulls out, resting his head on my shoulder. I feel his seed dripping out of me as I hold him there while he comes down from his high. Finally, he moves setting a kiss on my collarbone and stepping away to zip up his pants, "Are you okay?" For some reason his words make me blush, as if he didn't just do the most unholy of things to me. I move to pull up my pants, ignoring the forming trail down my leg, "Yes."

He moves beside me to rinse off the vibrator before putting it and the remote in his pocket. I turn to the mirror, and I remember where we are again, "We totally ditched your friends?" He smiles, holding his hand out for me, "They'll forgive us."

I take his hand, and we leave the bathroom; the bar is in full swing as if time never stopped for them, as if no one had a single clue. Daniel and Caleb are right where we left them, they're in the middle of a game holding a couple of beer bottles. Caleb grins as we approach, "Hey, there's the happy couple! We thought you guys forgot about us!"

Heat flushes my face as if he knew exactly what we were doing, but August ignores him, "Are you going to hand me a cue, so you can get your ass kicked, or are you going to keep running your mouth?" All three of them get excited as I happily step aside to watch. I've played before, but I'm definitely not good at it and don't intend on embarrassing myself.

12. Halloween gives you baby fever

"Hurry Hazel, we've got to grab the kids in fifteen minutes!" Rachel yells from the living room. She asked me to help tonight with some of the church kids, she's taking trick or treating. I'm currently rushing to put on the face paint she gave me in the bathroom.

Though it's hard to focus as August is leaning against the threshold with a smirk on his face, watching me. I'm wearing a simple black dress with long sleeves and tights, as my black cat costume.

I quickly paint on four whiskers, two on each side, and a little black nose. Placing the cat ears on the top of my head, I finish by washing my hands and that's when August laughs, "You look adorable."

"Thanks." I say unenthusiastically, moving to leave the bathroom. He moves out of the way, following me into the living room where Rachel waits. He picks up my phone off the end table, handing it to me, saying, "Call me if you need anything and please be safe." I roll my eyes, "So bossy." I take my phone out of his hand, "I'll see you later."

The night breeze whips our faces as Rachel and I head out the door, August watching in the distance. Rachel's dressed as an angel; wearing a white headband halo, a white fuzzy sweater, and dark blue jean. "So, we're just taking out a few of the younger kids that need adult supervision," She explains, starting the car and getting on the road. "Sounds good to me," I reply happily.

It doesn't take us long to pick up the kiddos, and I watch as Rachel comes to life interacting with them. We park in what looks like a popular neighborhood. The spooky décor lights up the streets as we hear laughter and excitement all around. The cool air runs up my legs as I get out of the car.

We unload the kids, and the oldest one is dressed as Batman, one as Cinderella and the youngest is dressed as a fairy. Rachel locks the car doors reaching for the hands of the oldest two saying, "Okay guys, let's hold hands as we cross the street!" I smile squatting down in front of the little fairy.

She's waving around a little wand and babbling words I don't understand, "Do you want to go get some candy?" Excitedly she yells in agreement. So, I smile more, holding my hand out to her, "Okay let's go show them how beautiful your costume is!"

She nods her head, her black hair barely covering her eyes as she reaches for me. Her little hand falls in mine and I stand hunched over, her feet tap against the pavement as we slowly follow behind Rachel and the other kids.

As we catch up with the others at the door, I stand three feet behind them with Rachel as they ring the doorbell. We don't take our eyes off of them as I say, "You seem good with them." The door opens and they yell trick or treat.

An older woman holds a bowl of candy in one hand as she reacts to their outfits, smiling and handing them a few candy bars each. She laughs, "You think this is good, this is just one of the families I work with, just wait until I have all of the kids in one room, that's when the real fun starts."

"So, you work part-time at the diner, *and* you run the youth group for the church?" I ask. We watch as the kids say thank you and begin walking towards us. "Yeah, it's a lot, but I love being around them, plus some of the parents are over the moon for the extra help."

As the kids reach us, the one dressed as Batman holds up a cherry lollipop to us saying, "Look Rachel, this one is my favorite!" She smiles down at him, "That's awesome, let's go get some more, shall we?" They scream in agreement, running to the next house. Rachel's eyes widen, "Hey, okay guys, wait for me!"

The youngest is standing still focused on trying to bite open a mini chocolate bar. I laugh, squatting down to her level, "Want some help opening it?" She nods her little head, almost shoving it in my face, "Open please." Her please sounds more like peas so I laugh again, "Okay, let me see it." I hold open my hand and she drops it in my palm.

I flip it being careful not to touch the wet bite marks as I open it, handing it back to her. "Thank you," she says, sounding like she said tank you instead. Shoving it in her mouth, she reaches for my hand and starts bobbing her head happily, we continue following her siblings.

The next hour or so we go door to door, and I try to keep my heart strings together as we pass more babies with their parents, experiencing their first Halloween. Baby fever will creep up on you in the weirdest moments, I swear.

The youngest one eats more chocolate than I think her parents will be happy about and the oldest two are proud their candy bags are full to the rim, each offering Rachel a piece to say thanks.

After we drop them off, we're back in front of August's house in no time, "Thank you Rachel, I can't believe how much candy they were able to get in an hour." I unbuckle my seat belt as her car idles. "Yes, well let's hope their parents don't kill me the next time they see me."

I look to see August opening the door to stand on the porch, and I laugh rolling my eyes. "I guess I better go, my *parent* is clearly waiting for me," I say sarcastically, and she laughs while waving goodbye.

I quickly get out of the car, and skip up to the porch, "Did you miss me?" Faking a pouting face he says, "Terribly." I smile and he steps aside letting me walk in and shutting the door behind me. He asks, "Did you have fun?" I nod sitting on the couch, "I did."

He smiles, "Good." He walks past me towards the kitchen, "I made dinner." I hop up following him into the kitchen, the aroma of baked chicken floods my nostrils, "Smells good." I move to sit at the table, as I watch him over the stove.

Soon he's setting a plate of baked chicken over white rice and broccoli in front of me. My mouth waters as the sight and I notice a bottle of Mwenzi Wine sitting on ice in the center of the table.

"What's the special occasion?" I question as he moves to grab the bottle. "There's no occasion, you need to eat, and I like to cook," he says, pouring a glass for the both of us.

I stare contemplating on picking at him more but he sets the bottle back down and moves to grab his knife and fork. So, I leave it alone, all too eager to taste the food in front of me.

August waits until I take the first bite to eat. When I do, lemon pepper and garlic romance my taste buds, I moan in delight, "Oh this is good." He smiles, moving to take a bite, and we enjoy the meal in silence.

When our plates are nearly empty, August pours us a second glass of wine, "There's been a minor security breach at work, they want me to review the footage in person for the report. I want you to come with me." I reach for the glass, "But I work at the diner tomorrow."

"I know. I already called in for you," he says downing his wine.

"You did what?"

He doesn't respond, we both know I heard him clearly. I push up from the table, standing as frustration heats my face, "You can't do that August. I only work there two to three days out of the week as it is, barely a few hours at that!" I move to pace the kitchen. "You know you don't need to work there," he says moving to stand in front of me.

I point my finger at him as he approaches me, "It doesn't matter if I need to!" I do, actually, but I don't tell him that, "You don't get to control my life August!" He places his hands on my shoulders, "I'm not trying to control you. We've already established that Little Bird."

I yell crossing my arms, "Stop calling me that!" I swear I see a smirk forming on his face as he says, "Why? Would you prefer little *brat* instead?" His hands move around my waist, and I move to press my hands against his chest in protest. He continues, "It's fitting, no? Rachel told me you dreaming of what's out there. Is that what the birds have, that you think you don't? The freedom to dream, to fly?" My face scrunches at his words.

I finally push away from him, and he lets me go. Why the fuck would Rachel tell him that? I speak quietly, "You don't want *me* August, you want to *own* me. You want to *control* me. I don't want to be controlled." He continues, his face falling in defeat, "I'm not trying to control you, but I won't lie, and say I don't like being in control."

He sighs, walking away from me, "When our parents ruined our lives. They took so much more from me. That first year, fighting became the norm. There wasn't a single day of peace or calm. I wasn't lying when I said I wanted to run away. I felt helpless, hopeless, and so fucking lost. Being in control, disciplined, that gives me stability, it makes me feel sane." He finally turns to me and whatever fuse that was lit inside me had diminished, and I realize my father didn't just fuck my life up, he destroyed August's life as well.

I look down briefly, twirling the ring on my left finger, I sigh saying, "Let's go to bed." I hold out my hand to him, letting his vulnerability linger in the air. He doesn't want to control me but is still controlling, so no matter what, this cage is still a cage, right?

I decided to go for a run this morning after August left for his. Truthfully, I don't know this area well but the plus side is we live by a shit ton of trees so I'm sure there's plenty of trails to choose from. I'm still pissed at Rachel for running her mouth. I mean, I thought she was a girl's girl, and I gave her my herbal tea! I didn't even tell her about the plane ticket so how does she know I want to leave?

I can hear my heart rate in my ears as I find myself running on a random trail. I normally take my earphones, but I think I misplaced them; however, the sound of early morning birds and nature is comforting. The smell of wet earth fills my noise as I jog deeper into the trees.

I finally start to slow down as my chest begins to burn and deeper breaths become harder to take. Controlling or not August has been kind to me since we've been married, so with his admission last night, I plan not to be such a brat today.

Which means joining him on his trip to work. He's head of the security department at his job. I wonder what that looks like, and I immediately laugh trying to picture August behind a desk of cameras dressed in security clothes. I take another thirty minutes enjoying the peace before I decide to head back.

A thin layer of sweat covers my body as I walk through the front door and a voice I haven't heard since our wedding day startles me, "There you are darling I was getting worried; you haven't called or anything! I thought maybe August did something to you and got rid of the body!" She laughs as I shut the door behind me. "Mom?" I question in confusion.

She's sitting on the couch wearing an expensive sweater dress and jacket. "What are you doing here?" I ask looking at my phone to check the time. I've got 45 minutes before we're supposed to be leaving.

"No, hi mom how are you?" She pauses waiting for a response I don't give her. "Well, if you must know, I came to collect you for the day, I've been dying to talk to you since you've been married!"

She says dramatically and I move further into the room. I'm not sure if August has made it back or not.

I reply, "Sorry I can't, August and I have somewhere to be today." She waves her hand dismissively, "Oh don't be ridiculous, I'm sure you guys can reschedule; after all I am your mother."

My heart rate spikes at the thought of still having to be her puppet even after being married. Was this marriage just a move across the board for her? I am still her pawn. "I don't want to…" I begin trailing off because I don't know what else to say. She speaks for me, "It isn't a matter of what you want, Hazel, please we've been through this."

Before I can respond, August emerges from the bedroom fixing the cuff on his suit, "Careful Carla, that's my wife you're talking to." His voice is silky smooth, but the threat doesn't go unnoticed. She meets his gaze sitting up a little straighter, "August! I didn't hear you come out of the room!"

He doesn't entertain the warmth in her voice as he responds walking over to me, "Yes well, I've heard enough from you, and I think it's best you leave. After all Hazel, and I have somewhere to be." He kisses my forehead as I feel rooted in place, unable to speak.

His response makes her smile disappear momentarily before she stands, "You're right, it's not right of me to show up unannounced." She stands heading towards us, I move out of the way of the door, "I'll see you two lovebirds at church, love you, Hazel." She waves as she heads out the door, and I finally take a deep breath.

I turn to August, and he's looking at me attentively, "I don't want her coming back here." He looks back at the door before saying, "Noted. Are you okay? You kind of froze up, there." I sigh, "Yeah, I'll be fine. She acts like that all the time." I realize I'm still in my leggings, and he's basically ready in a nicely fitted black suit, "Shit, I need to get dressed."

He smiles following me to the bedroom, "Wear a dress." I raise an eyebrow going straight to the closet door, "What kind of dress?" He stands in the doorway, sliding his hands in his pockets. I was planning on wearing one of my skirts, it's his job, so I'm certainly not trying to draw attention to myself. He smirks, "Do you have something purple?"

That's a specific request. I throw my hands on my hips for a moment before a dress comes to mind, "Is lavender okay?" I shuffle through the hangers before pulling on a mid-length long sleeve lavender dress. The front goes down into a v shape, having small slits on each side to expose just a bit of my legs. Long ruffles hang from the sides, giving a pretty mermaid look.

He nods, not moving from the door. "You're going to watch me change?" I question moving to take the dress of the hanger. He smirks, "I am." He's seen me naked before, but his words still send heat to my face.

I try not to sexualize myself as I undress, but I can't help it, knowing his eyes are on me, drinking in my every movement. He watches me every second, every move, I feel the heat spread from my head to my core by the time I've finished putting on short heels and brushing out my hair. "Ready?" I ask breathlessly, only then do I allow myself to look in his direction.

He's still standing there well composed, but his eyes have a wildness to them, and a beautiful budge imprints his dress pants. He straightens, holding out his hand for me, "As soon as we get home, I promise I'm going to devour you."

13. It's not a sex club

AUGUST

I've never been so pissed off for having to attend to work duties my entire life. If those fuckers didn't screw up last night's audit report, I could be screwing Hazel right now. She looks like a Goddess, torturing me with how sexy she is in that dress.

I'm pulling into the lot when she pulls me from my thoughts, "August, this is a casino." I take a deep breath as I head towards the back of the building, "I know, I work here." Her jaw drops before she asks, "Why do you work at a casino?"

I pull into the employee parking garage, stopping to scan my ID, "Because I enjoy it." That's not entirely true, but she'll find out soon enough. "You are full of surprises, you know that?" she says readjusting in her seat. I smile in response because she truly has no idea.

We park quickly, and I get out to open her car door. She places her hand in mine, and I guide her inside. The front of the building is on the opposite end, still the smell of cigarette smoke fills the air as we walk in. This entrance is not as dazzling as the main one, but still you can tell it's luxurious by the wide entrance, the white walls with gold trim, and the large expensive paintings that hang on the walls.

It's significantly warmer here, as I guide Hazel through the break room to clock in, and I immediately regret it. The two auditors, Ben and Jake, are sitting in the middle of a conversation when their heads snap up at our presence, or should I say hers.

Their eyes widen, and I move my hand lower down her back pulling her closer to me. *She's mine, assholes.* "I want you two in my office in fifteen minutes," I say as I move to clock in on my phone, while heading to my office. "In here," I say, pulling open the door for her and turning on the lights.

She looks around the room and laughs, "Somehow I'm not surprised by the black and white aesthetic in your office." I smile glancing around; it's minimal and not distracting, I see nothing wrong with it. I head over to my desk, and she lingers around the room for a moment. I start up the computer glancing at her every few minutes. As soon as I log into my email, three new ones await. I click into the one with the attached file and begin reading through it.

When I look up again, I'm taken aback by Hazel's beautiful round ass bent over on display in front of me, my dick pulses and I gulp.

I already know she's looking at the stupid award Daniel gifted me for Christmas. Sure enough, her voice lights up the room, "Biggest Dick Award?" She picks up the bronze penis, turning around to face me, "Should I be jealous or something?" I laugh sitting back in my chair, "It was a joke." She doesn't look entertained as she huffs setting it back down.

"Come here," I say sitting up. She moves towards me around the desk saying, "Oh, am I allowed to see your top secret security work?" A smile spreads across my face at her sarcasm, and she stops just beside me resting her hand on the back of my chair.

My face is all too close to her pussy, and I can't help my dick pulsing as I move to rub my hand on her ass, "We're probably going to be here a while, would you do me a favor and grab us a coffee from the break room?" She gives me a look of uncertainty but agrees and leaves the room.

I sigh, I need to speak with those knuckle heads and try and resolve the issue, and if I kept her here, they would be gawking at her instead of paying attention to me.

It's been no more than ten minutes into emails when my phone rings and I answer, "What?"

"What up asshole," I hear Caleb's voice through the other end. "I'm at work, what do you want?" I place my phone on speaker, setting it down to finish responding to emails. "Well, isn't that a coincidence. I was wondering if I'd see you at the box today." I frown, "I'm not bringing Hazel to the box." Besides, the only thing we can agree on is that she's a brat. Other than that we haven't talked much about our dynamic.

There's also the fact that she already thinks I want to own her, which I do, but not cage her in. "Are you sure about that?" The tone in his voice has me raising an eyebrow. "By the looks of it she's already found her way here?"

Snatching the phone and standing I bark, "don't play with my Caleb." He laughs, "Wish I was bro, better hurry. She looks like a lost puppy, don't want any of these fuckers getting any ideas." I'm already rushing out of my office by the time he hangs up the phone.

It's not like she's going to be ambushed or anything, but the box is our own little showroom, we gamble, drink, and most of all we show off our pets. A place where like-minded individuals can be themselves and enjoy their lifestyles out in the open. If she sees something she doesn't like, the hope of our marriage lasting is doomed.

Caleb is also right, that ring on her finger means nothing in there. I rush into the hall connecting the employee area to the private rooms. I sent her for coffee, how the Hell did she find herself in this section.

Quickly, I make it to the last door at the end of the hall. This section is mostly private rooms, so foot traffic outside of these doors is at bare minimum. Finally, I take a deep breath before entering the room.

Immediately, the sound of soft jazz fills the atmosphere. The walls are painted black, opposite the main halls, with gold trim and soft lighting around the room. There are few tables full of men and women playing poker with their pets or subs at their side or even at their feet. I can't imagine what Hazel thought walking in here.

There are waitresses carrying out wine or champagne to some men chatting over cigars near the couches. There, I spot Celeb sitting nearby with a glass of champagne and Kim kneeling at his feet. Celeb meets my gaze, and a smile erupts on his face, "There he is!" he muses, "Good ole pastor boy!" I ignore him, frustration filling my veins by the second, "I don't have time for your shit Caleb. Where is she?"

I glance around the room, an irrational fear of Hazel wrapped in someone's arms and being persuaded by their bullshit crosses my mind as Caleb says, "I saw her walk in the direction of the mini bar, by the looks of it, I'm not the only one who's noticed her." He waves, signaling Kim to move into his lap, "Better hurry. Our good friend Robert's already trying to make a move on her." I frown following his gaze behind me.

I see Hazel sitting at the mini bar as Robert is taking the seat next to her. I move towards them, not bothering to respond to Caleb. Once in earshot I hear her say, "Oh, I'm not here alone." She smiles at him before noticing me as I approach, relief flooding her face.

"There you are," I say, immediately place my hand on her lower back and turn to Robert as if I didn't notice him, "Robert, didn't see you there, how are you?" He takes a second looking at us before responding, "I'm doing good August. I didn't know you'd be here today, let alone with such a pretty pet."

I can't tell what's going through Hazel's mind, but I feel her tense beside me, "It's always good to see you Robert, but I'd like to have a word with her alone?" I ignore his statement as I'm sure Hazel will want an explanation. He laughs, "Don't be too harsh on her, my friend. I'd love to see her again!" I ignore his words, trying to not let them irritate me.

As soon as he walks away Hazel speaks, "He said you'd find me here." I turn her around on the stool to face me, and grip her thighs in my hands, "Who said that?" She nods her head towards the sofas, "Caleb did. As soon as I walked in, he saw me and told me to wait here for you. He said you'd know exactly where I'd be."

That fucker, always playing games with me, "And you believed him?" I squeeze her thighs, getting irritated that she trusts anyone other than me, best friend or not. "Well, you're here aren't you?" She shrugs her shoulders.

"I sent you for coffee. How the fuck did you get here?" I ask. She rolls her eyes, and I squeeze harder on her thighs. She winces before rushing out, "I don't know! I was trying to find the doors to the main area but wandered down some hallway when I saw someone walk through this door, so I just followed them."

I sigh, moving to pinch the brim of my nose. She continues, "So are you going to tell me why that guy, Robert, called me a pet and about this apparent sex club?"

I look around again and see a few men and women staring at us before responding, "It's not a sex club. Come on." I step back holding out my hand for her, and she raises an eyebrow crossing her arms. I'm not leaving her here by herself, there are too many gawking and curious eyes. I sigh, losing my patience, "I'll explain it to you, but first I still need to deal with work, then if you want to come back, we will."

She finally places her hand in mine, and I take her back to my office where I instruct her to sit and wait. Just as I predicted, Ben and Jake weren't paying attention to a damn thing I was saying.

Finally, after dealing with them, fixing the problem, and writing them up, Hazel is practically bouncing with curiosity. "I want to go back, but first I have questions," She states as soon as Ben and Jake leave my office. I power off my computer before leaning back into my seat, "Of course you do."

She moves to sit across from me, and I frown at the distance. "So, this sex club," She begins. "It's not a sex club," I cut her off to clarify. She rolls her eyes, "Well whatever it is, you and Caleb are a part of it, and Robert called me a pet, so it's clearly some type of club."

"You're right. We call it the box. It's a BDSM club, invite only of course. A bunch of Doms, Dominatrix, and other dynamics started this club a couple years ago. We used to meet somewhere else until I noticed our property rarely used these rooms and helped relocate it here. We have parties and play poker and show off our…different dynamics."

"My God, so you really are a Dom, aren't you? You know I can't be that for you, right? A pet? How does that even work?" She begins. "We've established that, Little Bird, you don't listen very well, remember?" She snaps, "Be serious August. *A pet?* What you want me to crawl on the floor to you, let you put a collar around my neck, and drink out of a pet bowl?"

"Something like that," I say more to myself but it's clear she heard me. I take a deep breath standing and walking around my desk to lean against it in front of her, "I want to own you Hazel, but I don't want to clip your wings. I want to collar you but only to show the world that you belong to me."

She raises her left hand showing me her wedding ring, "That is literally what this is for August." I smirk, "Not in my world baby." I lean over her, pulling her chin to look up at me, "Will you be mine in this world too, Mrs. Forkhill?" Her eyes are round and watery as she stares into mind, a million thoughts dance behind them but she only tells me one, "I don't want to wear a leather collar like some house pet August."

I speak softly still locked in our gaze, "It doesn't have to be, you can have a more subtle one. They're known as day collars." She bites her lip, still looking up at me and my dick pulses from the action, "I want to go back to the box, only because I'm curious. I'm not saying yes, August." I smile, kissing her forehead because she might not have said yes, but she didn't say no.

14. Confessions

August is holding my hand as we walk all the way back to the black box. I'm nervous but it's too intriguing to pass up. When we walk in the light in the room is dim, August drops my hand, and slides his arm around my waist, pulling me close.

I didn't notice before but there's a makeshift stage, where a woman dressed in a sexy latex outfit is standing over a man who's on all fours, with a mask and collar on. I whisper to August as he continues to guide me, "I thought you said this wasn't a sex club." He responds, "It's not, however people like to put on shows. Some are exhibitionists."

He guides me back to the lounge area, where Caleb and Kim are still seated. "Glad to see you brought her back." Caleb says as we sit near them. August doesn't respond and I glance at Kim who's kneeling in between Caleb's thighs like a literal pet.

The sight doesn't bother me as much as the thought of her being that way for August. She doesn't move or even blink as I stare. Suddenly, jealousy of their history begins to irritate me. I turn my focus back to the stage, and August move to whisper in my ear, "She's a Domme, she likes to put on shows for us quite frequently." Hmm. "Is that her sub then?" I whisper back. He nods in response as we watch the Domme continues to whip her sub.

After every lash, she encourages him to count, and by the count of ten she rubs his ass through his black briefs and then whispers something in his ear. I turn to look at August and he's watching me intensely.

Not saying anything, I turn back towards the stage, and she moves a stool center stage and is instructing him to stand up and lean on it so everyone can see his face. Intrigued, I watch as she pulls out a black strap on dildo from a nearby box and is now lubing it up. My God is she really going to peg him in front of *everyone*?

She answers my silent question by stepping behind him and in seconds he's grunting in pleasure. It feels like the atmosphere has changed, I feel hot, and my palms feel sweaty, yet everything else in the room has gone unchanged. There are a few other people watching like it's a casual performance, others are still occupied with their games and drinks.

My attention is brought back to the stage as she starts striking his back with the whip as she moves in and out of him. When did she pick that up? Suddenly I hear August's voice in my ear, "Are you okay, Little Bird?" I take a deep breath, nodding slowly. "Are you turned on?" he asks, still in my ear. I nod again as my face flushes with heat, is it that obvious?

I feel like I shouldn't be. "Does watching turn you on, or are you fantasizing about being up there?" I roll the idea of people watching me in my head. But it doesn't strike my interest, in fact, I think I'd be too embarrassed to enjoy the experience. "Watching," I finally whisper in response.

I begin to say something else when I notice Caleb staring at me, when he sees me looking, he says, "You guys hungry? Let's go back to my place, and we'll order take out." August stands beside me saying, "Maybe another time, I am ravenous right now but not for takeout."

He holds out his hand for me to take, and I feel flustered. Great, August, what a way to tell everyone how horny I am. Taking his hand, he leads me out of the dirty little black box sex club that's not a sex club. "That was interesting," I say as the door closes behind us. Looking at him, I ask, "Have you ever performed before?" He laughs still guiding me, "Not my style baby."

As he leads us back into his office I move to lean on his desk as he closes the door. "I want to collar you, Hazel," he states, surprising me a little. I hear the lock of the door before he turns walk towards me and I shake my head, "I can't August, I can't *be* that for you."

He stops right in front of me before responding, "I'm not asking you to be anything other than mine Little Bird." He moves to cup my face in his hands, "We can work out the kinks, okay?" I sign melting into him and repeat his words, "We'll work out the kinks."

He smiles before planting a soft kiss upon my lips and saying, "Turn around." He steps back, and I stand, taking a breath before turning around and resting my hands upon his desk, "Now what?"

A millisecond goes by before I feel his hand press me further down, until my breasts are flat on the surface, "Now, I get to admire you." I feel his fingers pull the bottom of my dress up and over my ass until my cheeks are exposed. I protest, "August you don't have-" He spanks my ass, shutting me up with a gasp. "I believe I owe you three spankings, Little Bird."

He doesn't wait for a response as he dishes out another, I jump at the impact being harsher than the one before, I let out a breath as the sting spreads, melting into me like butter. I hear the sound of his hand connecting with my ass again before I feel the sting of a stronger impact spreading through me and straight to my core.

"You're doing such a good job baby," August praises, and my pussy pulses in response. The final blow is the hardest one, earning a hiss from me as I close my eyes and wince letting the pain settle before opening them. August moves to kiss the now raw skin before saying, "Fuck, your ass is so beautiful."

And being the brat that I so clearly am, words full of faux venom fall from my lips, "You lied to me, you said three spankings and I counted four." As I am still laying on the table, he moves to speak in my ear, "Is that so? Well, allow me to confess my sins and pray for mercy."

He sinks to the floor behind me, pulling my panties along with him. His voice begins so lowly I have to focus on his words to hear him, "Forgive me, Father for I have sinned."

I feel him plant another kiss on my left cheek, "It's been far too long since my last confession." He slowly slips two fingers inside me causing me to gasp, "I confess two things to you today, father."

I can't tell if he's being serious as I feel his forehead rest on my ass, and his fingers begin a slow torturous pace, "I've lied to my beloved, a vow I promised not to break, forgive me father." I bite my bottom lip to keep a moan from escaping, unsure if August is lost in his words, or me. "Lastly, a decade ago, I gave my soul to you. Today I confess it was never yours."

"August please!" I whine cutting him off, as his fingers continue their agonizingly slow pace. He kisses my ass again before removing his fingers, and I sigh in anticipation of his cock. Instead, he moves, gripping my ass and burying his face in my pussy. I yelp at the sudden contact before my voice turns to liquid as I feel his tongue explore my lips.

"August," I moan his name weakly as he moves to tongue fuck me. "Oh yes," I whisper, moving my hands to grip the edge of the desk, as my legs begin to feel like Jello. His tongue is warm inside me, and I hear him hum in pleasure before he moves further down to lick my clit. I let out an unheavenly moan as I feel pleasure build in my core, "August, *please!*" My pussy is wet and ready for his cock, and he knows it, I'm starting to think he likes hearing me beg.

I squirm underneath him as his tongue speaks in languages only our bodies understand. He doesn't stop until he's pulling an orgasm from the depths of my soul. August finally stands saying sweet nothings over me, "You're such sweet wet girl, Hazel."

I moan in response, desperate to feel him inside me. He rubs the head of his cock against me saying, "Would you like to feel what you do to me, baby?" He inches the tip inside as I whisper, "Yes, please." I'm still trying to catch my breath, and he pulls out, making me gasp in frustration. He grins saying, "What's that, Little Bird?"

I finally scream, "August! *Please,* stop teasing me and give me your cock!" With a satisfied growl he sinks back into me, pausing momentarily to grip my hips before setting a toe curing pace, "Do you see what you do to me Little Bird? Can't you see how bad I want you, how bad I need you?" I'm trying to listen to his words but the pleasure for his body is too distracting. Is he really choosing right now to express himself?

I try to form a response, but his grip tightens on my hips as he slams deeper into me. It's like my brain won't work properly. All I can focus on is the overwhelming feeling of his cock inside me and his soul trying to etch itself in mine.

"You want to spread your pretty wings, baby? You want to see more of the world and do all things you've never done before? That's fine, you can have whatever you want; I just want you."

For some reason, my heart tightens in my chest, and I try to respond between moans, "August, no, please stop." He doesn't know what he's saying, he's just caught up in the sex. His stroke slows, reaching his climax and he responds through gritted teeth, "Baby you're not hearing me, I can't stop, and we both know you don't want me to." Suddenly I feel his dick pulse inside me, but he pulls out, and I feel the warmth of his cum over my ass.

I ignore the little disappointment of him pulling out as he quickly grabs some tissue from his desk to wipe me clean. Finally, I'm able to stand as he helps pull down my dress. When I turn to look at him, he pulls me close saying, "Come on let's go home." Let's go home? So, are we not going to talk about anything you just said? "Okay," I say instead of voicing my concerns, I'm feeling too tired anyway, at least for now.

We quickly find ourselves outside of the casino, the sun is setting, and the breeze of the air is turning into a shiver as he guides us back to his car. Silently he opens my door before getting into the driver's seat. My eyes begin to feel heavy as he starts the car and turns on the heat. He seems content which brings me back to the thoughts of his confession.

"August," I whisper sleepily. He looks at me briefly, raising an eyebrow, "Yes?" My voice is barely over a whisper as I'm losing the fight to stay awake, "Did you mean what you said?" I finally close my eyes, moving my head to rest against the seat, still listening for his voice. "I meant every word, Little Bird."

15. Sunday Dinner

AUGUST

Hazel's fingers have a grip on my left hand. We're sitting in the front row at the church and my mother is sitting on the opposite side of her. You can't tell by her face, which is glued to my father on stage, but this agonizing grip she's got on my hand lets me know she's irritated or at the very least uncomfortable. I don't know if she's worried about her mother, who I haven't seen today, or because my mother has tried to engage in conversation about grandbabies twice this morning.

I glance at our hands; does she realize she's squeezing so hard? I move to whisper in her ear, "Deep breaths, Hazel baby." She does as I say, taking a deep breath and her hold on my hand loosens. I move my arm, throwing it around her instead and pull her close to me.

Turning my attention back to my father he says, "Every day is proof we're living in the final days. God will return and take his rightful place! But the question is, are we ready for his return? Are we holding ourselves accountable?" He's using his pastor voice as I hear 'amens' and 'praise God' erupt from the crowd behind me. The rest of the sermon goes by in a blur.

As usual at the end of each sermon Larson and I stand beside my father as he says goodbye to the crowd. "Hi boys, do you have a moment?" My mother calls us. "Are you and your wives busy today? We'd love for you guys to come over for brunch; I'm making grilled cheese and tomato soup!" She chimes. I glance over at Hazel who's talking to Rachel with a scowl on her face, I sigh,

"I don't know-" Larson cuts me off, "Can't. Rachel and I will be busy all this afternoon!"

Her face falls a little at his response, "That's okay dear. I suppose you and Rachel should spend the day trying to make babies." Larson suddenly chokes on his own breath. She turns back to me, her eyes hopeful. *Thanks Larson.* I sigh ready to decline but she pouts, "Please son, your father would love the company."

I mentally groan before responding, "Sure, we'll head over after going home to change." Her face lights us with glee, "Perfect!" I feel Hazel approach behind me and my mother pounces on her, "Hi Hazel! How are you doing Hun?"

She moves me out of the way as she pulls Hazel into a hug, "We were just talking about lunch! Of course, I'd love for you guys to stay for dinner!"

She releases her but keeps her hands on her arms as she continues, "You know your mother's told me you make the most amazing marinara chicken bake! I'd love for you to come over and whip it up sometime!"

Hazel tenses in response but smiles, "Um." She pauses, looking over at me, and I give her a reassuring smile. "I don't like to cook," she says, stepping out of her grasp and moving closer to me.

Hmm, maybe some time around my parents is more needed than I realized. "Oh, that's okay. Well, we'll see you guys in a bit then." I nod, "Later mother." Turning to Hazel I ask, "You ready to go?" She nods and we leave the church.

On the car ride home, Hazel is too quiet, "What's in that mind of yours Little Bird." My eyes are focused on the road, but I see her glance at me through my peripheral vision. She speaks quietly looking out the window, "I was just thinking back to when my mother wasn't so bad. I know the crap with our parents turned my mother's heart to coal, and I spent so much of my life hating your mom for it. It's funny though because she's technically my mom now too."

She sighs and I glance at her as we approach an intersection. "I thought for sure when I got married at least I'd gain a mother that would love me." I press the gas and she takes a deep breath, "Instead, I have a mother that uses me and another I loathe."

I try to understand her perspective before responding and truthfully, I can. I'm not sure how I'd react if I had to be around her father. "Would you like to cancel?" I ask the only acceptable thing because what do you say to that. She shakes her head, "No, we already said we would go. I'll be okay, thank you for understanding though."

I reach over to squeeze her thigh in reassurance, "I can't speak for my mother's character, but I'd like to think she doesn't *loathe* you." I smile at her, and this time she rolls her eyes but I see her smirking.

Once we make it back home, we change into more comfortable clothes and are out of the house in ten minutes. The drive to my parents' house isn't normally long but I'm letting Hazel drive and told her not to go over thirty-five miles. "Hazel, please keep both hands on the wheel," I beg noticing every time she uses one hand, the car swerves. "Fine," she whines placing both hands on the wheel, "but I want to go faster." My heart rate picks up at the idea, "Baby steps Little Bird."

I try to cool her down from her excitement. She's doing good on her turns and getting better at breaking early enough, but we've only practiced a handful of times. As good as she's doing, the idea of her speeding is only making me picture her crashing and my heart clenches in my chest. I take a deep breath, shaking the image from my head, "Very small baby steps."

We make it to my parent's house with all of our limbs and a very proud Hazel. She slips her hand in mine, after handing me back the car keys. "Ready?" I ask once more. She smiles in return, and we walk to the front door.

My father must have been watching, because the door swings open before we reach it, "Hazel, August! Glad you guys made it! August son, Do you think you can help me move something in the back real fast?" I look over at Hazel, who slightly nods and smiles, "Sure, Dad."

He moves to pat my back before turning to Hazel, "We'll be right on it, Lisa's setting the table, I believe, go ahead and let yourself in." Hazel doesn't respond as she continues to the open door. My Dad's hand is still on my shoulder as we head to the side of the house, "So how's the married life son?"

He opens the side gate before I respond, "It's good, she hasn't tried to kill me yet." My dad laughs as we continue to the back of the house. "She pregnant?" he asks bluntly. I groan, "Dad come on, not you too."

He throws his hands up in defense as we stop in front of his woodwork shed, "I'm just asking, you know your moms going to pester her about it at the table." I shake my head knowingly, "Of course she is."

He finally unhooks the lock and says, "I built this bench for your mom since she wants one for the back patio, now that we have a real chance at grandkids." I shake my head again, getting frustrated, "Really? If Larson heard you said that he'd be pissed, let alone Rachel. They still have a chance; they still have a very real possibility of having kids."

He sighs deeply, "I know son, but they've been trying for so long now. I haven't lost faith but forgive me if you being married has brought out a little more hope in your mother." Looking back towards the house I shake my head, saying, "Whatever you say, Dad. Are we going to move this thing or what?"

He moves inside the shed saying, "That *thing* is hand carved Indian teak wood that took 53 hours to carve." I laugh, woodcarving is definitely his end goal, "Yeah okay." We position ourselves at each end and we left when he counts to three, waddling it all the way to the back porch.

We dust off our hands, and he says, "There's been something I've been meaning to ask you about." I take a seat on the bench we just placed, "Oh boy, here we go." He sits down with me resting his hands in his lap, "Look son. Larson told me about a conversation Rachel and Hazel had awhile ago. Now I don't care much about the details but word of advice, no matter the situation, if she wants to go, you let her go."

I shake my head, hating how words travel in this small town. "She's not going anywhere-" I try to say but he cuts me off. "I know, but August, listen to me. It'll hurt a Hell of a lot less if you let her go, then try and keep her somewhere she doesn't want to be." He responds, double tapping my shoulder before giving it a light squeeze. I bite my tongue, "Okay dad."

Suddenly the sliding door to the house opens and my mother steps outside, "What on God's green earth is taking you so long?" My dad stands, "We're coming woman." He looks down at me and nods as I stand up behind him and follow them into the house. "Thanks, mom, for having us for lunch," I say as I spot Hazel already sitting at the kitchen table.

Lunch is laid out at the center and glasses of water sit in front of us. The table feels much larger now that only four of us are seated. "Are you okay?" Hazel asks as I take the seat on her left. My parents are pulling in chairs across from us. "Yeah, I'm good," I respond as my father quickly says grace and we begin filling our plates.

My parents are more entertaining than I give them credit for as they talk about stories from their youth. I glance at Hazel every so often to see if she is enjoying herself. When we've finished socializing, the sun is setting, and Hazel follows my mother into the kitchen to help put leftovers away.

"It was great having you over, son," my father says handing me his glass. "Yeah, it's nice" I agree, moving to bring the last few dirty dishes into the kitchen when I hear the pop of a wine bottle. I pause beside the archway out of sight.

Hearing my mom's laugh she says, "I'm serious Hazel, I am more grateful for you than you know." I hear the sound of pouring wine and Hazel responds, "I understand, really I do, but forgive me if this all takes a little getting used to."

"I can do that, I respect your decision, Hazel. Despite everything that's happened though, I'd do it all again if it led me right to this moment. Cheers, to new beginnings," My mother says, and I hear the sound of wine glasses clinking before I decide to step in view.

"Sounds like an after party happening in here?" I smile and surprisingly Hazel's not tense. "Yes, well it's only wine, dear," My mother says right before taking a sip. I see Hazel sip hers as well as I move to set the dishes in the sink. My mother holds up the wine bottle asking, "Would you like a glass?"

I immediately shake my head, "No, it's getting late, and I have to drive." Hazel's eyes widen at this,

"I can drive!" She beams and I laugh, "But you've already started drinking, Hazel baby." I move to grab the glass out of her hand, "Come on let's go home." She pouts but we say our goodbyes and the car ride home is peaceful.

"I'd really like a shower," Hazel sighs, moving sluggishly as we make our way through the front door. "Okay, go get your pajamas, I'll run the water." She heads to our bedroom without another response as I walk to the bathroom. I roll up my sleeves, turning on the showerhead and quickly adjusting the temperature. Soon, Hazel walks in with her hair now neatly wrapped in a green bonnet. "The water's ready," I say as she begins undressing.

My eyes rack over her body, and she bites her lip saying, "Can we watch a movie after? There are still a few hours before I'd like to go to bed, and I'd really like a warm cup of hot chocolate." She steps in and I nod as I begin undressing myself, "Hot chocolate sounds good." I step into the shower after her, and I focus on washing up before my dick stirs and leads my brain.

She'll still inside the bathroom when I head to the bedroom in a towel for a pair of pajama pants, socks, and a long sleeve bed shirt. When I return from the bedroom, I see the bathroom light is still on so I head to the kitchen and grab two cups, milk and two creamy hot chocolate packets.

After a few moments of busying myself with making our cups, I hear Hazel call from the living room. I guess I didn't hear her come out, "What do you want to watch?" I grab a spoon mixing the now hot cups as I respond, "I like action movies, but I'm okay with whatever you want."

Finally, I carry the cups into the living room where Hazel is sitting on the couch in a velvet red pajama set. She's scrolling the tv before saying, "Is a kid movie, okay?" She looks up at me as I hand her the cup, and I laugh nervously, "What kind of kid movie are we talking about?" I place my cup on the end table before joining her on the couch, her body is still radiating heat from the shower and the smell of her body wash makes my dick jump.

She responds, "How about talking cars?" I reach over for my hot chocolate, before throwing my arm around her saying, "I'm game for talking cars." She smiles quickly putting on the movie and nuzzling under me.

A good thirty into the movie my phone dings with a message and at first, I ignore it but then it rings again, and Hazel lifts her head to face me and says, "You can check that you know." I pull her closer to me, "No, whoever it is can wait until the morning. Besides this movie is good." She smiles, laying her head back against me.

A few scenes go by, and I feel my eyelids getting heavy. When I look down at Hazel, her eyes are already closed, So I kiss the top of her head, and rub her shoulder whispering, "Let's go to bed, Little Bird." She stirs a little, letting out the cutest little hum. Her eyes are still closed as she speaks softly saying, "Mmm okay."

She sits up, and I stand holding out my hand for her. Her eyes open just barely as she places her hand in mine. I smile, she's so cute when she's sleepy. Turning off the tv, I lead us back to the bedroom and we quickly wrap ourselves in bed, falling asleep.

*"Just like that baby," I moan looking down into Hazel's beautiful brown eyes. I'm sitting on the edge of the bed and she's sucking my cock like her life depended on it. Fuck, I can't get enough her. She comes up for

*air saying, "Please August, please fuck me." I do as she says, pulling her up and into the bed. Hovering over her I say, "I'm going to fuck a baby into that pretty little pussy of yours." She moans in response as I quickly line and sink myself into her. "Would you like that Little Bird? To be full of my cum?" I ask nearly coming from the feeling of her walls around me.**

Suddenly I wake, quickly realizing we're still in bed. Fuck, I was dreaming. I groan, reaching down towards my rock-hard cock, then blink my eyes to adjust to the darkness around the room. I look over at Hazel, who's still fast asleep, and the idea of filling her up with my cum and seeing her belly swollen has me pulling back the blanks and moving to hover over her.

I begin to pepper kisses down to her pussy and she stirs under me, "Mmm August?" Her voice is soft and barely over a whisper. "Shh Little Bird, I just want a taste," I say before my tongue finds the split of her lips. The smallest of moans leaves her lips, but her eyes are still closed. "August," she says my name, but nothing follows as I focus on wetting her enough to slide in.

Her brain might be sleepy, but her body responds to my touch as she wiggles underneath me, soon rubbing to create friction against my tongue. She whispers something about cock, and I rise, moving too quickly to slide inside of her, "Fuck baby." Feeling her warmth around me, I begin to move in and out of her saying, "Look at you, taking my cock in your sleep baby."

She moans quietly as her eyes flutter open for a moment but close again. "I'm going to come in this pussy of yours, Little Bird. Would you like that?" She nods squeaking out her pleasure. Her pussy feels so good I close my eyes momentarily groaning to the image of her pregnant again. I feel myself about to come as my cock throbs inside of her and I hear her suck in a breath, "come inside." She doesn't finish her sentence as another quiet moan leaves her lips.

Soon my pace waivers as I feel myself spilling inside of her. "Fuck yes," I groan, stroking out every drop. "You're such a good girl, taking all of my cum," I say still inside her. Her eyes open like little slits and she says sleepily, "I like being a good girl." My dick pulses a final time before I pull out of her.

Hazel starts to move to get out of bed, but I wrap an arm around her saying, "Where are you going, Little Bird." She whispers, "I need to clean it out." I shake my head even though she can't see me and say, "Stay in bed; we'll clean it in the morning." She doesn't move for a moment but must decide she's too tired to care because she does indeed snuggle back in bed. I pull her closer to me and she's fast asleep before I can whisper goodnight.

16. Stuffed Bunnies Can Protect You from the Chaos

The sound of August's phone ringing wakes me from my sleep. I lift my head, and I can't tell if it's still the middle of the night or early morning. He groans, moving to answer it. "You better have a good-" He begins but is cut off by a voice on the phone that I can't hear.

"Woah, woah, woah. Slow down, what do you mean?" He says confused. A few seconds of silence pass before he responds suddenly getting out of bed, "Don't panic. I'll be on my way, call Daniel too." I hear him shuffling around the room and in the drawers, "Don't jump to conclusions, I'll be there soon. Meanwhile don't touch anything. In fact, don't even move."

I finally sit up as he turns to me now partially dressed, "I'm so sorry, Little Bird, I have to go to Caleb's. I don't know when I'll be back." He kisses my forehead and leaves the room before I can respond.

I wait as I hear him shuffle down the hall and soon through the front door. I suddenly have the urge to pee as I register the extra wetness between my legs. I try replaying August's sudden urge for sex, but it plays back in my mind like a fever dream.

I stand heading to the bathroom still sleepy as feel liquid slid down my leg, shit, he really came inside me, *and* I slept in it. Fuck. I move to the toilet, pee and take extra time to wipe whatever I can out before willingly going back to bed.

The sun is up before I am, and I tumble out of bed desperate for a cup of coffee to wake me up. I have a shift at the diner today, so at least I'll be busy. I shoot August a text, asking if everything is okay, considering the frantic way he left last night. My coffee's ready in no time, but I still get no response from August. Ignoring it, I take my cup back into the room and decided to get ready for work.

Rachel picks me up, and we arrive at work in no time. She tells me about the fertility blend and how she's got Larson drinking it too. I only respond with brief replies allowing her to fill the conversation most of the car ride. I confronted her about filling August with misinformation, and her excuse was she thought I sounded unsure and thought I'd cheat on August. I'd leave before I'd do something like that to August. In fact I am leaving, but no one needs to know that. Anyway, I told her I forgave her, but I just know our friendship will never be the same.

Work is quite busy when we arrive, we quickly clock in and begin taking orders and serving coffees. I'm getting into a flow as I help customer after customer, I'm even beginning to recognize our few regulars like Joana. She loves her coffee to arrive after her club sandwich, so she drinks it slower and has to have three packs of sugar, never more, never less.

The morning rush is just beginning to die down as I recognize a face that walks in. "Justin? Oh my God, it's great to see you!" I say as Justin walks in dressed casually in blue jeans and a caramel-colored hoodie. "Hi Hazel! Its goods to see you too!" He strides over towards me, as I wait behind the counter. "What are you doing here? Can I get you anything?" I say leaning casually against the counter. "Oh, I just stopped by to grab a bite, but I'd love a fresh cup of coffee if you have the time."

I look over to see Rachel watching as I respond, "Yeah of course!" I move to grab the pot and a cup before pouring him a cup in front of him, "What'd you have in mind to eat?" He beams as I set the cup in front of him and hand him a few packs of sugar, "Good ole hot cakes please!"

I set the pot down and turn back to tease him, "Hot cakes? Lord, you sound like Cathy." He smiles adding sugar in his cup just as Rachel walks up, "Hey Hazel, isn't it time to take your break? I can take over for you if you want?"

Is she serious right now? "No, I got it, I was just about to put his order in. I'll take my break in a few minutes." I respond curtly. She lingers a moment looking at Justin before looking at me, "Kay, just, let me know if you need me to cover." I nod, "Okay."

She glances between us once more before leaving and Justin responds, "Sorry, my guess is you're not supposed to be talking to me." I quickly shake my head, "No, it's just." I roll my eyes, taking a breath, "I'm married to her husband's brother so, you know." I shrug my shoulders, but he doesn't seem bothered saying, "Ahh I get it. How's married life anyway?"

I smile, "It's eventful, nothing that I'd ever imagined, that's for sure." He takes a sip of his coffee, "Oh, I bet, glad it's *eventful*."

"Yeah. Well better get your order in. Don't want Rachel calling my husband on me," I say moving towards the back. He quickly states, "It's good seeing you, Hazel." I nod, continuing to walk away.

The rest of my shift goes by in a blur, Justin doesn't stay that long, and Rachel doesn't question me about him after. On the ride home, I double text August my shift was over and a question mark, I'm not sure I like him not responding to my text.

I think about calling, but I don't want to talk in front of Rachel. When we arrive in front of my house, she cuts off the car wanting to say something, but I beat her to it, "I'd appreciate it if you didn't look at me with judging eyes. Justin is just a friend, Rachel. Nothing more."

"But-"

"But nothing, do you think I am my father, Rachel? Do you think I'm seriously going to *cheat* on August?" I say with my hand on the door handle. She takes a moment to respond but says, "No, I don't think that of you, Hazel."

"Good," I respond, pulling the door handle and stepping out of the car. "I'm sorry, I didn't mean to insinuate that. I just care about our family, very much." I shut the door ignoring her response, "Later Rachel."

I quickly head to the front door fishing for my key, not paying attention to see if she left yet. When I open the door, I'm taken aback by the tall figure standing in my living room.

The figure turns around to face me, "Hazel Marie Grace." I'm stunned. My father calls me by my maiden name. I speak slowly, "It's Hazel *Forkhill*." Am I hallucinating? Is that really him? His features have aged, that black short fro I remember is now a mix of salt and pepper, he's even grown out a mustache.

"What the Hell do you think you are doing? marrying yourself off like some hussy?" He doesn't move from his spot. I frown, "Excuse me?" He responds, "Your mother told me you came back to Springville and married August Fucking Forkhill? Are you out of your mind?"

I swear I'm about to crack a laugh of hysteria but instead I back track, "I'm sorry she told you I married him? Like it was my choice?" Suddenly my mother emerges from my fucking kitchen, "Hazel dear, don't act so clueless." This time I actually do laugh, "Oh my God. Pause what are you doing here? I don't see you for years and suddenly you show up demanding an explanation from me?"

My mother moves to the living room as if all of this is normal, "And you? Did you call him? Did you know where he was all this time?" She rolls her eyes, her tone high pitch as if she really is trying to help, "Hazel, stop being dramatic, of course I called him, I didn't know what else to do?" I turn back to him shaking my head, "Of course that's what she told you. This was her idea. marrying me off to August to rid herself of me."

She speaks over me, "Hazel, don't be ridiculous!" Now my father turns his anger towards her, "I don't know what game you're playing woman! Using our daughter for your bullshit games! You said she hated me and never wanted to see me! You've been messing with my head the whole time! This is why I left your crazy ass!" Suddenly they're screaming at each other, yelling back and forth. My ears begin to ring, and my breaths become shallow.

I slump against the door behind me but the sudden movement of my mother walking to the hall gets my attention. I follow her still hearing my dad scream at her from afar. When I turn into the only open door I the hall, she's in our bedroom and immediately starts throwing clothes from the drawers into my old suitcase.

"What are you doing!" I say moving to try and stop her. She snaps at me saying, "Hazel if you don't move your fingers, I will break them!" I gasp, pulling my hands back in shock. She's never threatened me with violence before. I watch her continue to throw my clothes, "Why are you do-ing this? You made me marry him. Didn't you get what you wanted?" My throat clogs as tears threatens my eyes.

She glances at me and laughs, "Oh Hazel don't be such a baby. People get married and divorce all the time. I thought August would understand that you are mine. What I say goes, but it's clear he thinks otherwise so, I'm taking his little toy away."

Suddenly, I feel like that little girl hiding in my room, trying to drown out the noise of their chaos. My eyes water, and I can't see anything but the little girl clutching her stuffed bunny, while squeezing her eyes. The scars on my thigh somehow feel like they're burning, itching, dying to resurface, begging to bleed.

"Hazel!" I hear my father's voice yank me from the void, and I realize I'm now in my mother's car, while they bicker in the front seat. When did I get here? Where are they taking me? He continues, "Did you hear me? I am taking you to a lawyer and you are signing divorce papers."

I don't respond, I feel like I can't why do I feel so small around them. I pull out my phone to try and drown them out and I see my text thread with August is still sitting with my unread messages. I text "Cupcakes." The message soon shows delivered and I wait and wait but nothing happens.

So, I send it again and again, until it suddenly creates a chain of the word. August please, please, please help me. "Hazel, dammit I'm talking to you!" I feel myself falling into the void again as my body goes on auto pilot.

I don't register a thing until I feel my father folding a plane ticket in my hand, "Go sit down." He dismisses me and I listen, why am I listening? How did we get here so fast? I sit down at the near-est set of chairs. Trying to wrap my mind around the events happening around me. My phone pings and I remember messaging August. I pull it out, his response is *almost there* and the one previous to that says *on my way*. I must have not heard it when it pinged the first time.

My mother walks over to me saying, "Don't look so terrified Hazel, this is for your own good. At least with her father, I can still call you when I need you. Plus you two have a lot catching up to do." She tries to touch me, but I move my head. She frowns, "You've always been an ungrateful little girl." She balls her fist at her side before turning away.

My father approaches me then, a familiar scowl on his forehead, "Don't worry, we'll get far away from here and you'll never have to see your mother again." My heart clenches in my chest, August. What about August?

As if summoning him with my thoughts, I hear his voice from behind my father, "Get the fuck away from her!" He shouts, getting my father's attention, as he nears, he cocks his arm back and punches him in the face. I wince at the sound of the contact.

My father stumbles and August pushes him out of the way immediately pulling me to my feet to embrace him, "Are you okay, Hazel baby?" Suddenly I feel like I can breathe.

I take a deep breath, "I'm okay." My father stands turning to August, "What do you think you're doing!" Shades of red I've never seen on skin, color August's features, "Taking my wife back home, that's what the fuck I'm doing." August suddenly pulls me behind him, and I notice a crowd forming. I hear my father say, "She's not your wife, this was a mistake!"

"What? You've come to take my wife from me too, asshole. Was taking my mom not enough?" I think August is preparing to swing again, but two security guards are quickly intervening, "That's enough you guys need to vacate the property, now."

Finally, August turns back to me sorrow now painting his features, "No need, we're leaving. Come on, Hazel baby." I don't even look back to see the mess left of my father as August guides us out of the airport.

My heart feels like it's beating again as he holds my hand all the way to his car and goes as far as opening my side and bucking me in. When he joins me in the car, he lets out a sigh and I say, "Thank you for showing up, August."

"Thank you?" He repeats shaking his head. "You don't have to thank me Little Bird. I would have showed up a million miles to wherever you were, I'd never stop trying to find you. As I've said, you are mine, baby." He raises my left hand to his lips, before planting a kiss and lacing our fingers. I hear his words, and I relish them for a moment as he starts the car.

The car ride back is silent, and I keep replaying everything that's happened in my head. I keep trying to process it all but that burn, that desperate need to silence the fog is screaming at me. So, I move to pinch my thigh, hard enough to hurt but not so August will notice. The fog seems to clear, my pulse calming, as I take a deep breath. Focusing on the ache forming under my fingertips.

17. Scars

The afternoon sun is still out when we make it home. Walking back into the house feels odd, like I hallucinated the whole thing, and my parents were never here. I take a seat on the couch and August heads to the kitchen.

I hear the clinking of glass before August comes back with a glass of water. Sitting next to me he says, "Here." Taking the glass with no hesitation, I take a sip and the water somehow gives me voice, "She wasn't supposed to come back here." I feel him move to rub my lower back, "I know, and I'm so sorry."

That itch on my thigh comes back as I try to say, "I can't stand her. I can't deal with her anymore, August." My voice falls remembering what my father said about me never wanting to see him, about the lies she told him. August must see this discomfort in my face as he asks, "How can I help you, Little Bird?"

My voice falls as I say, "I don't want to be in my head, I need to…" The image of my scars bleeding fresh has me taking a breath and trying to grasp the feeling from the thought.

"Okay," August seems to understand as he stands holding out his hand for me, "Come with me." I set the glass down, and he helps me to my feet, not letting go until we reach the threshold of our bedroom.

Moving to the ottoman at the end of the bed he says, "I need you to take your clothes off and sit at the edge of the bed, can you do that for me?"

I nod, doing as he says, removing first my work pants and top. I see him open the ottoman revealing itself as a chest which surprises me, but I don't say anything. I sit watching him as I remove my bra, and he pulls out neatly wrapped black rope, two long white candle sticks, and nipple clamps.

Discarding my panties as well, my breath catches in my throat as he closes the secret chest and moves to place everything down beside me, but the rope. "Tell me your safe word, Little Bird." He begins unraveling the rope, as his eyes rake over my body. Looking into his eyes I say the word that somehow feels stronger between us.

He takes a deep breath, "I want you to keep your eyes on me, don't want you getting lost in that pretty head of yours." With the rope fully unwound, I nod, "Okay." He steps back, "Stand up and place your arms behind you." I move slowly doing as he asks, and I see him smirk before he plants a kiss on my forehead. Once my hands are resting behind me, he turns me around to face the bed.

Slowly he begins wrapping layers of rope first around my breast, crisscrossing the rope a couple times. The feeling of the rope against my breast feels tight but not uncomfortable. I feel him tying a knot behind me before the rope wraps around my shoulders, once, twice, and a third time before I feel him tying another. Soon I feel wrapped inside the rope, and it's oddly comforting. Like this rope is holding all the pieces together, keeping me safe.

I let out a soft sigh of content when I hear the sound of him tying two more knots and tugging to make sure it's secure. When he finishes, he asks over my shoulder, "How does that feel?" I wait for panic to rise or discomfort but I still feel content, so I say, "It feels nice."

He lays me on the bed, face first. I rest my head on the left side of my face as I feel him straddle my ass. His fingertips follow the rope up my spine until he leans over to speak in my ear, "Can you count too ten Little Bird?" Count to ten, okay. I can do that. "Yes," I whisper, almost ready to ask why. "Good, I'm going to spank you, and I need you to count with me, okay?"

I nod, and he leans back up. His hands rub over both of my cheeks before he dishes out the first spanking. The impact is a tease, nothing compared to what I desperately want. "Are you counting Little Bird?" He asks.

"One," I say quietly, he dishes out another. "Two," I breathe, still in need. The third strike is harder, but I want more, "Three." The next two are back-to-back, "Four and Five." I feel myself getting wet from the feeling of his cock hardening against me, combined with the growing ache on my ass.

This smack makes me tense, a small sting spreading through my cheeks, "Six." The impact of the next one makes me gasp, the sting more intense and lasting. I feel him rub his cock ever so slightly against me causing my pussy to pulse as I say, "Seven."

My ass is feeling more sensitive as the next blow makes my body jerk and tears swell in my eyes, "Eight." He swings so much harder; I'm sure my cheeks will bruise as my body jerks again underneath him, and a small cry leaves my lips.

"Let it out, Little Bird," August coos and I could make him stop, but I don't have to, I don't want to. All I have to do is count, "Nine."

My ass feels like it burns, and I take a deep breath as we reach our goal. The pain spreading through me is enough to make the tears fall as I feel it spread from my cheeks, through my body, and to my core. "Ten," I barely manage through blurry vision as the tears finally fall on my cheeks. August moves to kiss the impacted area, "That's a good girl."

My eyes are still wet as he rolls me over, and my ass sings in discomfort from the pressure. "Would you like a cupcake, Little Bird?" August asks moving from atop of me and checking my reaction. I know he's asking if I want to use our safe word. Feeling comfort in the pain and arousal I reply, "No, thank you." I breathe through my silent tears as he takes in my response.

He grabs a candle stick and lights it, asking, "Where do you feel the most pain?" As the flame catches, I watch as he waits for my response. "My chest," my voice breaks as I respond honestly, and he moves the candle right above my heart. As the wax falls on my skin, the pain sizzles, and I hiss as my head falls back momentarily allowing the pain to coil through me.

"Eyes on me, baby," August says. I feel the wax hardening on my skin as he's moved the candle upright. When my eyes land on him again, he asks, "Where do you *like* the most pain?" I glance down at my thigh responding, "Where my tattoo is." He moves the candle downward, and my body reacts to the wax again burning and cooling into my skin. "Tell me what it says," He asks not letting the candle up as the wax begins to cover the ink.

I'm not sure if he already knows and just wants to hear me say it or not but my voice is choppy as I focus on the words through every drip, "You, are enough, a thousand, times enough." Still not letting up the candle, making the burn last through the building layers of wax he says, "Say it again."

This time, I bite my tongue and choose to relish in the pain, but it stops, he stops. August asks, "Do you want me to stop?" I shake my head, tears welling in my eyes again. He doesn't respond as he blows out the candle and a small wave of disappointment courses through me. He lays the now melted stick down and grabs the chain of nipple clamps.

Hovering over me, he finally speaks, "Then tell me what it means to you?" I take a deep breathe, looking up at him, "It means, I am enough." I begin and the pain in my chest causes tears to fall, but I continue not breaking eye contact with him, "A thousand times enough."

Finally, he moves, clamping the ends onto my nipples and squeezes, earning a cry from me, "Good girl." August moves to kiss my forehead, and I realize his cock is hard against me, "I want you to say it, until you come, do you understand?"

"Yes," I nod, and he pulls me to the edge of the bed, hovering over me, so that he can still reach the chain of the nipple clamps with one hand and play with my clit with the other. "Say it, Little Bird." He demands, and I do.

I repeat the words, and he rewards me by pulling the chain and impaling me at the same time, the pleasure from the pain and his cock makes me gasp. "Again," He doesn't move until the words fall from my lips and again, I am rewarded with a tug at my breast and him pulling out and sinking back into me.

We continue like that until the words fill the room, along with the sound of our bodies connecting, and the pain scorching through my nipples. Soon enough, I feel the strongest orgasm wash over me and I attempt to arch my back, but the secureness of the rope and August on top of me has my withering in place.

As I come down from the high August release his hold on the nipple clams and focuses on his stroke inside me, "You're such a good girl, baby." He continues sweet praises until he's coming inside me with a loud wave of his own orgasm.

He lays on top of me, kissing all around my face before pulling out and rolling over to untie me. Free from the bindings, my body feels oddly exposed, but August quickly pulls me into bed, and I feel a different type of ache in my chest. One that's warm and calm. One that feels safe. I want to voice this but the fatigue I feel along with the comfort of August's embrace has me whispering something short and sweet, "Thank you." I feel him kiss my head in response as I drift off to sleep.

"Please don't leave," I beg from the kitchen table. August smiles, placing a cup of coffee in front of me, before sitting beside me with his own, "I wish I didn't have to, but they need me." I roll my eyes, ready to throw a fit if means keeping him here, "It's not fair, you're leaving for the *third* day in a row, and we're supposed to go to your parent's house to help prep for thanksgiving dinner!"

This past month has been full of August leaving to go help Caleb and Daniel, he hasn't told me why. It's infuriating. "Being a brat isn't going to make me stay, though I really wish I could. At the very least I'll be back before tomorrow morning."

"Tomorrow morning!" I whine crossing my arms in a huff. He seems amused by my frustration, "You want me to be perfectly fine with you leaving to go help Caleb when you won't even tell me what's wrong!" Doesn't he see how unfair this is?

He sighs as his phone begins to ring, "I've already told you, the less you know the better. I'll explain as soon as it's safe too." He leans over to me, his phone still ringing, to kiss my forehead. I sigh in defeat as he begins to lean away, but I quickly pull him back to me to kiss his lips.

He kisses me back passionately, giving me just as much urgency. I bit his bottom lip tasting him, and he bites mine back harder. Can't he see bad I want him to stay. His phone's no longer ringing and August pulls away feeling the shift of energy in the room and I beg one last time to no avail, "Stay with me."

He rests his forehead against mine saying, "Hazel baby, now what kind of friend would I be to leave them, when they need me most?" He leans back as I answer, "A shitty one, but you'd be my shitty one." He laughs at this, finally standing and redialing whoever called.

I feel that ache in my chest again, the one I want to devour me whole, and bask in its peace, but I'm not ready to tell him that so instead I say, "Come back to me." He smiles back at me as the line answers, and he makes his way to the front door.

I sigh, deciding to finish off my coffee and check the app of the new cameras August had installed earlier this month.

Not that we think something bad is going to happen, but neither of us felt comfortable after both of my parents made their way into our home, without notice. Since then though we haven't heard from either of them, nor have I seen my mother anywhere around town. Now that I'm acknowledging it, I don't think I've seen Thomas either. Not that I'm complaining, he's probably realized she's too toxic to love and left.

Before I know it, Rachel and Lisa are waiting out front, honking the horn. I quickly lock the door, checking the cameras one more time before getting into the car, behind the passenger seat where Lisa sits. "Hi, Hon!" Lisa's excitement fills the car as she greets me. "Hi, Lisa! Hi Rachel!" I say, buckling my seatbelt.

Rachel replies, "Hi Hazel, I hope you don't mind, we're stopping at the store before heading back to the house. We need a couple of last-minute ingredients." Lisa chimes in, "And don't forget the wine!" Playing nice won't be so hard as soon as there's wine in my system, "Sounds good to me."

They hold small chatter in the front seat as I listen and only chime in when necessary. I text August, I miss him, because it's true. It's almost annoying how attached I've become to him, but he reassures me, he wouldn't have it any other way. When we arrive at the grocery store, he texts me back the same words, and I smile to myself.

Quickly, we find ourselves first in the produce section grabbing cobs of corn and premade macaroni salad. "Have you ever tried potato salad?" I ask as Rachel sets it in the basket. "I've tried it once or twice; I don't really care for it much." She unintentionally stabs me in the heart, and although I hate cooking. I might have to slide in a dish or two at these family gatherings. I mean come on, these are staple holiday dishes, I just can't *not* have them.

"Maybe I can convince you to try some homemade."

She looks at me sincerely, "I'd like that." We continue to follow Lisa around as she tosses different foods and snacks into the basket. Finally, we make it to the wine isle, and she holds up a bottle of Blackberry Mwenzi Wine, "Should I get one for today and one for tomorrow." At the same time that I say yes, Rachel says no, and we look at each other.

"Rachel?" Lisa says her name, her voice rising at the end. Rachel sighs, "Gosh darn it, I was trying to wait until tomorrow to tell everyone but, we did it, we're pregnant!" The excitement that explodes from Lisa draws suspicion from the bystanders. "Thank you, God!" She yells, nearly dropping the wine, which I happily take from her hands as she pulls Rachel in for a hug.

She pulls back and pulls me into the hug, surprising me, "I'm so blessed my family is growing!" I get out a small congratulations as Rachel and I both laugh a little uncomfortably. When she lets us go, her face is all red from joy and Rachel continues, "We had our first ultrasound the other day, Larson and I wanted to confirm the baby's beating heart before we said anything."

She pauses, taking a deep breath before continuing, "The bad news though the doctor has instructed I go on bed rest, immediately to keep the pregnancy viable for as long as possible." This makes Lisa scowl, "Rachel oh my goodness and you're here walking around with us, no, we can't risk it, we need to get you home asap!" Rachel tries to protest but Lisa is having none of it, "Nope, this is a gift, and we will not spoil it, Hazel and I can prep the food just fine."

After hurrying to the register, and getting back to the car, Lisa insists on driving now and I can only imagine if Lisa is acting like this towards her pregnancy, how will she act during mine.

Woah pump the brakes, not *mine*. Not *happening*. We stop at Rachel's, dropping her off before heading to Lisa's house. "Can you believe it? Praise God!" She celebrates some more on the drive. "I was so terrified it would never happen for them, and now that it has! Oh goodness, I can't wait to tell John!" I smile, "It's exciting." I should probably thank Cathy for tea the next time I see her.

I debate if I should tell August through text but truthfully, I'm not even sure if he'll believe me, or if he'll even answer. We make it to her house in no time and as soon as we walk through the door Lisa yells, "Rachel's pregnant!" We hear Johns voice from the backyard, and he comes stomping in through the back door, "Don't yank my leg Lisa Forkhill!"

"I wouldn't dream of it, John!" She beams at him as I stand to the side witnessing the magical energy between them. He rushes to her, pulling her into an embrace as he lifts his head to the ceiling saying, "Thank you God! Thank you!"

They start to dance and twirl, I almost forget what she's done. In fact, I wonder how she could have ever did it? They look so happy together.

"Mm-mm" I clear my voice, realizing I'm still holding some groceries. "Oh, sorry darling!" John says smiling and I move to the kitchen counter, "Where would you like all this to go?" Lisa begins to tell me where to place things and I offer to butter and pre-wrap the cobs. We begin to move around the kitchen in sync and I can't help thinking; this feels really freaking nice.

18. Missing girls and Secrets

I stare at the purchased plane ticket in my email. My flight's supposed to leave in two days. Another month has past, since Rachel's been on bedrest. I've been able to pick up more hours at work, making me reach my goal of enough money for the plane ticket, and then some. Yet, I don't feel the satisfaction I thought I would. I don't feel the desire to leave as much as I did in the beginning.

In fact, I feel the opposite, I want nothing more to breathe in every in of moment of August, that God will allow. Still though I expected to feel something when I finally made the purchase. Even now as I stare at it, I'm waiting for a thrill, butterflies in my stomach, a knot, *something*. Yet, nothing comes. I think back to when I called his home, our home, a cage. Was it ever one in the first place? Was August the one who actually set me free?

"Hazel baby, are you ready?" August calls me from the other side of the bathroom door. "Coming!" I yell, powering off my phone and turning on the sink to pretend to wash my hands. I rub them against my black dress and open the door to reveal a very tiresome August. He and Daniel have still been *helping Celeb*. Whatever that means, he still won't tell me a damn thing about it, and I'm getting sick of being in the dark. "Ready." I sigh, looping my arm in his.

Church on Sunday has become a routine for us, especially now that Rachel can't be present, John has been silently relying on us to be the church's coupled image. Larson's been showing up, but of course his mind is on his wife. August hates it just as much as I do. We sit in the front row as usual, hearing small talk around us as Pastor John makes his way to the front.

"Did you hear about her mother? I wonder if it's in the genes." I hear two girls whisper behind me. Not knowing exactly what they're talking about, I try to ignore them. As John begins introductions August places his hand around me pulling me into him.

Again, I hear the girls giggling behind me, "Oh, did you hear about that missing girl!" I finally turn, snapping at them, "Girls! If you can't be quiet, I suggest you leave!" They look at me appalled before sticking their tongues out and finally turning their attention to the pastor. I don't hear a peep from them during the rest of the sermon.

Now though I'm on the phone with Rachel as Larson, August, and John are talking to the lingering souls of the church. "Don't forget the waters and please make sure Larson sets the tables out right," Rachel says, sounding like she's moving something plastic around in the background.

"Okay Rachel, it's just tables. I'm sure he won't mess it up." I respond looking over to see the remaining crowd file out the door and John leaving with them. "I know I'm sorry I've been sitting in this house for a month now, I think I'm just going a little stir crazy," She responds laughing dismissively.

"Well, how long do you need to be on bed rest for?" I ask as I hear August walking up behind me. "Just until the first trimester is up." I feel him wrap his arms around me, so I say, "That's good, we'll we've got to go, I'll keep you posted, bye." I hang up, turning around in his arms. "Larson's already heading over to the pop up, you ready?" He asks. I take the moment to enjoy the soft look in his eyes, "Yes, I'm ready."

We stand there lingering a moment as his eyes hold me captive. I speak quietly saying, "You know, we could go home. I'm sure Larson can handle today's food drive all by himself." He smirks at this, "That sounds tempting, but then I'd have Rachel pissed at me, and you know what they say about pissing off a pregnant person."

His hands drop from around me as he offers his arm to lead us to the front doors. "No, I don't actually." I say, posing my voice high pitch and innocent. He only smiles as we head towards the doors.

Larson's got the whole set up ready by the time we arrive, which is remarkably fast considering we weren't that far behind him. Instead of socializing with the people in line August stands next to me, ready to help hand out food and water. The wagon beside us full of brown lunch bags tells me we're not serving hot food today, but food, nonetheless.

The line is growing antsy as Larson comes towards us with the last two cases of water from his car. "Ready?" August asks him as he places them down next to the other four. Larson nods in response and beckons the first people in line over.

We smile and move in sync as the first few people grab bags and say thanks. A younger woman with childlike features walks up though, tiredness shows heavy under her eyes as she smiles stopping in front of me, "Hi Mrs. Forkhill, I just wanted to say your presence in the church means a lot to me." She nods her head towards August as he helps with the next in line, "The way you and Mr. Forkhill have really shown up, not only as a strong couple but for the church is really inspiring, and I hope to one day find a man who not only loves me but God as well."

I smile at her trying not to think about August's occupation or hobbies. I know we both don't *hate* the church, but I think being raised in it has a higher bid on why we stayed, "Thank you, I'm honored we hold a high place in your heart. I hope love finds you in many ways in this life, not just in the form of a man." I smile and laugh hoping my response doesn't come off rude, but still hits home. She smiles in return, finally grabbing a bag and water, "I do too. Thank you."

After a while the line is almost gone, and I notice the two younger girls from the church this morning. They say thanks and take their food, which makes me wonder what they were talking about earlier. I move closer to August, whispering to him between people, "Hey do you know anything about a missing girl?"

He stiffens a brief moment before letting out a sigh, "Who told you someone was missing?" He's not denying it. I reply, "I heard about it." More people walk up, we say hi, they take a bag and leave. "Where?" He whispers back. "So, someone *is* missing?" I ask worry seeping through my voice.

As if calling on fate the town sheriff pulls up to the curb of the park. August and I watch, and I feel oddly unsteady. He doesn't approach us though until the line is gone.

"Hey August," He greets, and I'm surprised he calls him by first name. "Hi Robert, how can I help you today?" August says stepping towards him, I feel like I've heard that name before, but I roll the thought away as I pretend to clean up as I listen. "Nothing much, boss has me doing footwork about the missing girl, Kim."

Oh my God *Kim* is missing? He continues, "Other than that, no one's questioned it much and unfortunately since she's known about the company she keeps, everything is pretty tight lipped." What the actual fuck am I hearing right now? August sighs, "Heard anything new on Thomas?"

Robert replies, "Nah, he's still claiming it was an unlawful arrest and what not. He's got nothing though, and his lawyer knows it." Thomas having to do with Kim and her disappearance makes no sense. This must be a misunderstanding because how the Hell did that happen? Their voices get lower as I look up and see them moving back towards the cruiser. It's only then that I recognize the face of the man in uniform. That the guy from the black box who approached me at the bar, *Robert.*

As we finish cleaning up and drop the remaining supplies at Larson's house, he thanks us and by the time we make it home, I'm burning with questions that I'm unsure I'll get answers too, but dammit I'll try. "August," I call his name just as he shuts the front door behind him.

"Yes, Hazel baby," He replies, setting his things down by the table at the door and begins loosening his tie. "Are you going to tell me what the fuck is going on?" The frustration bubbles off me and he only sighs moving to sit on the couch. I remain standing to show him how serious I am, I need answers.

He runs his hands first through his hair, then down his face before saying, "Kim is not missing." My eyebrows raise in confusion and just as I was about to respond he continues, "She's dead." Heat feels like it drains my face, "She's…what?" Did I hear him right?

A horrible knot forms in the pit of my stomach and what makes it feel worse is that I didn't like her. Which makes me somehow feel guilty. I finally move to take a seat next to August. Turning to him I ask quietly, "Did Thomas kill her? Is he in jail?"

His brows knit momentarily, "What? No." This is too confusing, "Then why were you guys talking about him?" He looks at me a moment, what he's thinking I'm unsure, but he responds, "Thomas didn't kill her, and he's not in jail. He's trying to get a lawyer to get your mom out of a psych ward."

Okay, now this is too much information. Before I reply though he continues, "I had your mom arrested for breaking and entering our home. Then, I may or may not have had some papers forged and got her sent there."

His confession leaves me winded but yet, I don't feel any pity for her. "Wait so back up, if Thomas didn't kill Kim, then who did?" His lips press into a line and suddenly his phone rings. Of course, his fucking phone rings.

When he sees the caller ID, he debates a moment before answering it in front of me. "What, Daniel?" He snaps and I hold my breath to listen. "What do you mean you need to leave? No, I can't leave Hazel alone right now." My heart thumps in my chest and drops at the same time. Is he finally done with helping his friend, or am I going to be stuck alone again. He continues, "If you want me to do it fine, but I'm not bringing Hazel and I'm not leaving her alone right now."

After August's phone call with Daniel, he rushes to change, kisses my forehead and tells me he's going to be right out front and not to open the door for anyone but Daniel. When Daniel does come, he heads straight into the kitchen looking just as tired as August.

I follow him, maybe I can squeeze some more information from him. I wait and watch as he makes himself sliced apples and peanut butter. Normally, Daniel is bubbly, more enthusiastic, but the Daniel in front of me looks anything but. He hasn't even realized I'm standing here watching him.

"So," I begin. He doesn't look up from his task as he responds, "No." I frown, "What do you mean no, I haven't asked a question yet?" He finally turns to look at me holding a plate of apples in his left hand about to eat one in his right. He arches his eyebrow as he takes a bite and I use it as a sign to ask my question, "Why is Kim dead, and who killed her?"

He swallows before picking up another slice, "I'm not answering that." I am not liking this Daniel, what happened to frat boy Daniel? He was much more fun. I huff finally moving to take a seat at the dinner table as he continues to eat, leaning against the counter. "Are the police involved?" I ask.

"Yup."

Okay that's good, right. I sigh, "So it's being handled."

"Yup." He replies again, and now I don't feel confident in his answers. We sit in silence as he finishes eating, then pours himself a glass of water and moves to sit at the table across from me, "Look Hazel, I'm sorry, it's been a long day. If August hasn't told you anything yet, then it's not my place to. I'm ready for things to go back to normal, but until then." He lifts his glass, finishing off the rest of his water.

I don't reply, and we sit there in silence as he circles the rim of the glass until his phone rings. He sighs, answering it, "Hey Dad, I know I said I'd be there, give me another hour or so…Well, if you need to call your doctor, do so, I'll be there when I can." He hangs up afterwards and I know it's none of my business, but I ask anyway, "Is your dad, okay?"

He shakes his head shoving his phone back into his pocket, "Not really, apparently, he's got some cold, but he likes to exaggerate sometimes and anytime he thinks something is wrong, he wants me around. It's probably nothing, but the man has a fear of dying alone."

"Where's his wife?" I ask.

He sighs, "She died when I was young." *Shit.* "I'm so sorry," I say apologetically. He shrugs though, "It's all good, I didn't know her very well anyway." Momentarily he flashes a smile before standing to take his cup to the sink.

It's not long after that, when we hear August come through the front door. Daniel stands ready to take off but asks, "Everything good?" August shuts the door, nodding in response, "Yeah." We meet him in the living room. "Good," Daniel responds, moving past him.

"I'd love to stay and chat, but you know. You guys have a goodnight." Daniel doesn't wait for a response as he takes off in a hurry out the door. I really hope whatever's going on doesn't take a toll on him.

The sun is setting and August looks like he needs a shower and a three-day slumber. "Is everything okay?" I ask as he closes the space between us wrapping his arms around me. Taking a deep breath, he smiles, he actually smiles in relief, "I think it will be. Care to shower with me? Then I'll cook us a quick bite to eat." I cross my arms while still entangled in his, "You sounds like a man who just cheated on his wife and is now up to kiss ass."

I raise an eyebrow, and he laughs, "Never that, Little Bird." I stare at him for a moment wondering if he'll bring the conversation back up from earlier. Daniel said he'll tell me when he's ready, so I just have to shut up and wait. I sigh, before moving up to kiss his lips. He kisses me back, but I remove myself all too soon, "I'll go start the shower."

We fall into a comfortable silence as we shower and find our way into the kitchen. I find a glass pouring myself some wine as August begins raiding the fridge to put together a meal. Thoughts from today still ponder in my mind, so as much as I'd like to shut up about I can't.

So, I pick a topic he might tell me more about, "So, my mothers in an asylum." He's silent at first, and I fear I might have soured the mood but as he pulls out tomatoes, onions, a green bell pepper, and his cutting board he says, "Yes. Are you upset about it?" To be honest I should be, she's manipulative and controlling, but she's still my mom. Yet, I can't bring myself to care, "Not really, no. What about my dad though? You don't think he'll come back?"

"No, I delt with him too." He says, continuing to cut up the veggies.

This gives me pause, before I down the rest of my wine, saying, "He's not in some crazy house *too,* is he?" He laughs responding quickly, "No,

I told him to fuck off though. Maybe threatened him a little." I smile and tease, "So you threatened to kill him if he comes back?" He finishes cutting the onion without even flinching, as I'm sure the onion should be burning his eyes by now.

He moves onto the bell pepper, "I'd threaten to kill anyone for you Little Bird." He says it in a way that doesn't feel like a joke and sends butterflies down to my stomach. I move to pour myself a second glass of wine.

Soon the food is ready, and he's setting a plate of sauteed veggies and cut strips of medium cooked steak in front of us. The sides include mashed potatoes and gravy with canned corn. I thank him as he pours himself a glass of wine, and we dig in.

Later that night, I find myself locked in the bathroom again staring at the email I no longer know how to feel about.

19. A blessing for a curse

It feels like a breath of fresh air to be focusing on more important things like the pretty black girl sitting on her knees, naked and tied up in front of my desk while I work. My assistant pulls my attention back to the screen, but Hazel soon lets out a whimper and my eyes fall back on her.

I know she's suffering from that vibrator in her pussy and biting down on the cloth in her mouth to keep quiet, those nipple clamps are keeping her worked up too. God, she's such a sight to see, my cock is begging for this damn meeting to be over so I can stuff myself inside of my alluring wife.

I glance at the time, it's showing 4:32p.m. We have to be at Larson's by five for a family dinner and this meeting was supposed to be over an hour ago. "Vanessa, can you have the remaining key points of this meeting sent to my email?" I ask but my tone leaves no room for debate. She's baffled a moment but says, "Yes, I can."

"Great," I respond, and immediately close the video chat, then close the laptop. I look over at Hazel whose eyes are watery and begging. She's been acting really bratty today and I'm not sure why, but here we are. Ready to collect my dues.

I stroke my cock through my pants as I stand. Walking over to her nonchalantly. Once in front of her, the noise from her toy grows and I pull out the cloth in her mouth and she gasps. "Are you ready to apologize for how bad you've been today, Little Bird?"

"Yes." she pants. I squat in front of her, removing the toy from her pussy. When I do, she lets out a sigh, slumping a little. Turning off the toy, I replace it with my fingers to check how wet she is and fuck I can't wait to be inside her.

I whisper, "Such a pretty girl, all wet and waiting for me. Would you like me to fill you now?" I slowly move my fingers in and out of her, spreading her juices around her lips.

"Yes, please," She begs, and it almost sounds like a prayer. "Look at you, using your manners." I say, glancing up at the clock, showing 4:36p.m. I curse not having enough time to properly handle her, "Up we go then." I help her stand, and quickly move her to bend over my desk. "Unfortunately, we have to be quick baby. So, show me how sorry you are and make me come," I say as I pull down my zipper, only making enough room to pull out my cock and shove it inside of her.

She moans at the contact and as much as I want her to work for it, I feel myself ready to explode any moment. Nonetheless, I move painstakingly slow inside of her, and she whimpers trying to use whatever movement she has to create more friction.

"Tell me how sorry you are Little Bird," I say still moving slowly. "I'm sorry, I'm sorry for being bad today," she whines. I smirk, pulling out to move faster, she's so obedient when my cocks on the line.

I hold onto the rope to pull her harder into me, and I'm sure with nipple clamps still in place, the scrapping of her breast on my desk is giving her the edge that she seeks. "That's a good girl," I say and then I feel her pussy clench around me. Damn she feels so fucking good, I groan feeling that familiar tight sensation in my balls.

"Shall I paint your pretty walls with my seed baby, stuff you full of my cum until there's no doubt your womb is full?" I say stroking in and out of her. She moans, "Yes, August, please come inside me." I spank her ass, and she hisses a moan, making my cock throb. Within minutes I'm com-ing inside of her, and then I focus on making her come.

Soon, her orgasm begins to wash over her, she moans, "Yes August, I–" she stops as if not to say something, but then she continues, "I'm coming, oh fuck, August I'm coming!" I feel like I should point it out, but we really don't have the time.

After, I quickly unravel her, leaving us with no time to catch our breath. "We definitely don't have time to shower, do we?" she asks, still panting. I reply, "No not unless you want to hear my mother's mouth about us being late."

I leave the rope and nipple clamps on my desk, with a mental note to put them away later. Then, we both scurry to the room to quickly dress. Really, I just change my pants but we both douse ourselves with our fragrance bottles hoping to mask the scent of sex and quickly brush of our teeth and take gum for good measure. Soon, we're out the door and into the car, racing over to my Larson's.

When we arrive, my mom scolds us anyway. "You're late!" She says from Rachel's kitchen. "Sorry," I respond as we enter the house. Immediately I see my father, Larson, and Rachel sitting in the living room. "Hey guys," I say, Hazel says the same. After greeting everyone, my mother calls to Hazel, "Would you help me set up the table dear? Dinner is almost ready."

Hazel agrees, and I kiss the top of her forehead, joining the others in the living room. Sitting at the edge of the couch Rachel's stomach is a little more noticeable, and I can't help the image of Hazel pregnant clear in my mind.

It feels like a film flashing across my eyes, of her carrying our child, and the different stages of life that entails. Traveling wherever her heart desires, as long as I get to witness her happiness along the way. All the ways I could possibly punish her in one lifetime. Enduring whatever this life may bring with her on my side. It hits me like a car crash in my chest, and I slump into the seat.

No one seems to notice though, even as I look across the room, into the kitchen area now, as she's setting dish wear around the table. Smiling at something my mother's saying. My heart aches in my chest as I realize; I love this woman.

The evening with the family continued in a warmful bliss at my new revelation. After saying our goodbye, I respond to a text Daniel sent me asking me to come over. It's well into the night now, but Hazel said she's okay with it. So, I sent him an on my way text, and we drive over to his place.

Daniel lives in a small apartment closer to the center of town, near his dad's car mechanic shop. The heart of town always looks a lot spookier at night when there's not a soul around. Most of the shops only have a light or two, and nothing too bright.

I reach my hand over to the passenger seat and entwine it with Hazel's. As I do I glance over at her and she's quietly sleeping, and the sight makes warmth swell in my chest.

I know she wants to know about Kim's death, but I have to keep it under wraps a little longer until Caleb's mom, Cora, smooths out the fine lines. I'm still not sure what I should tell her, explain everything, or tell her nothing at all. I don't want her to bear the weight of that information anyway.

I half expected her to walk out on me when I told her about her mother, but to my surprise, she wasn't distraught about it. Which makes me happy I bought those cameras; I won't be letting that shit happen again.

As we pull in front of Daniel's place, I let him know I'm here, and Hazel stirs beside me, opening her eyes as she whispers, "Are we home?" I turn off the engine, looking over at her. I don't know what Daniel wants but I don't think it's important enough to disturb her, so I respond, "Not yet, I'll see what Daniel wants then we'll go home. Go ahead and rest, baby." She barely nods in agreement, and I lean over kissing her forehead.

Once I step out and shut the door I lock the car, just in case. Before I can even make it up his driveway, Daniel comes hurling out his front door, breathing like he can't inhale oxygen fast enough.

"Daniel?" I begin wary, I can't see his face from this distance in the dark. So I continue my approach like walking up to a wild animal, "You good?" He crosses his arms over himself shaking his head.

When I'm close enough, I see his eyes are bloodshot. Has he been crying? I stop in front of him, and he finally responds, "My dad…He has cancer." My stomach drops and as his words fill the air, tears force their way down his face.

"Fuck," I breath out quietly, trying to under-stand what I just heard. Disbelief wanting to take hold of my mind, because no fucking way. I reply, "Fuck, dude I'm so sorry." He stands there shaking his head clearly trying to fight back the tears.

So, I do what any other best friend would and pull him into a hug. We raise both of our arms around each other, and I say again, "I'm so fucking sorry, Daniel." Daniel has always been the happy, overly enthusiastic one of our trio, so seeing him like this unsettles me to my core.

I've seen him upset before, sure, but the absolute devastation I feel radiating from him has my throat feeling clogged and my mouth dry. Even when Caleb and I would bicker he'd be the one to crack a joke to ease the tension. My stomach knots in distress.

I feel him shaking and hear him sob onto my shoulder like it wasn't supposed to come out, like he's fighting back the pain. He pulls away within seconds, and my stomach knots more, "Do you want to talk about it?"

He nods his voice sounding raw, "Yeah, I, ugh. I kind of overreacted when he told me. He probably thinks I'm pissed at him." I quickly glance back at the car and say, "Let me take my wife home."

My heart rate pulses, hearing those words fall from my lips, my wife. but I clear my throat, I continue, "Then, I'll race back over, okay?" He takes a deep breath wiping his face with his forearm, "Okay." I look at him a moment longer before returning to my car.

Getting Hazel home is easy enough, she slept the whole way. When we arrive at home, I lean over kissing her forehead to wake her, "Hazel baby." She doesn't move at first. So, I get out of the car, coming around to her side. Even as I open the door, she barely seems to notice. I move, leaning over her to kiss her lips, saying, "Let's get you too bed, Little Bird." Her eyes are still closed as she whispers, "Don't go."

Her words create an ache in my chest and as much as I'd love to take her to bed, my best friend needs me. "I won't be long," I say, holding out my hand. Sluggishly, she takes it and I get her inside, quickly kissing her goodbye and heading back to the car.

After I race back over to Daniel and he's sitting on his porch step with a beer in his hand, I'm relieved to see he's calmed down a bit. When I approach him, he offers me a beer, and I take it sitting down beside him.

I crack it open and take a sip, The cool air around us makes the bitter liquid feel like a chill running down my throat. I sigh, waiting for him to speak first.

He takes a deep breath, takes another sip then finally says, "He has prostate cancer. He told me like it was no big deal." He takes another sip of the beer and his voice cracks as he continues, "He's had it for four years. *Four* years, and I never fucking noticed."

He takes a deep breath, and I ask, "Isn't it curable?" He scoffs, "Yeah, which is what I told him, but the man didn't want to go through all of that, saying he'd rather die. I guess he meant that literally." He throws his head back chugging the rest of the glass bottle. I do the same.

"Damn that man. I guess his stubbornness runs that deep." I reply, setting down my bottle. Daniel hands me another before grabbing another for himself, "Tell me about it. Even now, he's acting like nothing is wrong. Refusing to acknowledge it and going about his day like any other."

We work off the caps and tap our glasses together before taking a sip and I ask, "So what made him tell you after all this time?" He sighs, "Because now he's in stage four, which is the most aggressive. The cancer spread to his lungs, which is why he went to the doctors in the first place. He was complaining about chest pains."

We sit in silence redigesting the situation. Why does it feel like God has a way of blessing you and cursing you on the same day? Giving me Hazel, finally making Larson a father, and now threatening to take Daniel's dad away.

I shake my head taking another sip of the beer, which has my chest feeling warm inside and my head a tad loopy. Daniel breaks the silence again and changes the subject, "Do you still think it was an accident?" I already know what he means, so I respond more than confident in my answer, "The evidence proves so. So yeah, I don't think he killed her on purpose."

Daniel laughs in disbelief, "Man, I know you and Caleb were kinky sons of bitches, but this? What the fuck is breath play, and how do people get turned on by that shit? We're going to be so fucked if we're wrong." Daniel's into BDSM, but not on the same level as Caleb and I, which is fine, but I trust our best friend. I'd do the same for Daniel as well.

I jokingly scold him, "Not Daniel McCarter kink shaming. The man known for never fucking the same girl twice. When has Caleb ever held that over your head?" He kills the rest of his beer saying, "Yeah, well none of my kinks ever lead to someone's death."

"True." I respond because honestly that's all I can. I'd never lose control with Hazel in a way that would threaten her life. Babysitting what's left of my beer, I continue, "Still, I trust our best friend, The evidence proves Caleb killed Kim by accident during a kink session. We've already done our part so as long as his mom does her job correctly, the public won't get involved, turning it into something it's not." Daniel replies, "Doesn't it bother you, that she was your sub before his, and now she's dead?"

I roll the thought in my head before responding. It's unsettling, but I was never close to Kim. I definitely didn't feel for her the way I do for Hazel. I always knew our situation was temporary. Especially since she'd always seem more enthusiastic for sessions with him, even when the session left bruises. I finally respond, "She was never meant for me. It sucks that she's dead, but our relationship was never serious."

He nods in silence for a moment before reaching to grab himself another beer. He offers me one, but I decline, knowing I still have to drive home, and I'm buzzed enough.

Daniel finally responds, "I don't think you should tell Hazel."

"I agree." I say as my eyes feel heavy. We sit a little longer the silence, sobering before I take a deep breath and stand, "I better get home. Are you good, man?" He nods, "Good enough." I check for my keys saying, "Alright, I'll catch you later then. Call me if you need anything." He waves me off, and I rush to my car, rolling down the windows to keep me alert on the drive home.

When I pull into my driveway, I'm overwhelmed with comfort knowing Hazel's fast asleep in our bed. It's quiet as I walk through the front door. I lock the door behind, and check the lock on the back door, before checking the cameras.

I stop in my office to look over that email Vanessa sent me. As I'm reading the first two bullet points, a notification pops up on the bottom right corner. Looking at it, it says something about a flight reminder, so I click it, and I realize Hazel's email is still logged into my computer.

Her email fills the screen on my desktop and my heart drops to my stomach. It's a flight reminder for tomorrow with Hazel's contact information and a printable copy of the ticket.

She's leaving? She's…my thoughts trail off because how did I not see this coming. Haven't I shown her how much I want her. How much I want everything for her. Was she always getting upset me, not because she likes bratting, but because she genuinely doesn't want to be here with me? I sink into my chair despair and heartache blooming in my chest and making its way up my throat.

I glance at the rope still on my desk and a sinister thought of keeping her with me crosses my mind, but then so does my dad's voice. If she wants to go, you let her go. That's what he said to me that day at his house and dammit he's right.

20. His Little Black Bird

Last night, August woke me out of my sleep for sex, which I'm starting to think he likes fucking me when I'm barely conscious. I'm not complaining, though it was different last night. He was more sensual, I don't know, more intentional with his movements. Every kiss, every touch, every single thrust. My core heats just from memory.

August left for his morning run and normally he's back within an hour, but he's been gone since then, and I practically have the whole day to kill before I'm supposed to be at the airport.

I keep thinking the excitement will kick in. Maybe it's just delayed because I've been here so long. I dress in dark blue bellbottom jeans and a loose grey graphic t-shirt, nothing fancy today.

I pack in no rush, since I'm clearly alone, and decide to only take a carry-on bag. I finish grabbing my body wash and toothbrush from the bathroom, and I'm hit with the memory of August seeing my scars for the first time and how he vowed to protect me, even from myself. I sigh ignoring the weird feeling in my chest. This is what I want. I want to travel and not have to depend on anyone. Not stay home and raise babies.

Oh, but August's babies? Suddenly I can picture it as clearly as day, my body growing and changing with his child, a child made from love. I shake my head, God what am I saying. "It's not love," I say out loud to myself and to think I almost said I love you to him yesterday while he bent me over his desk. I mean he hasn't said he loves me either. No, this isn't love and it was never going to last. I have to do this; it's time to be independent.

Finally putting his number to use, I ask Justin to take me to his grandmother's shop since it might be a while before I get my hair done again. He arrives shortly and even though I feel odd leaving the house that's become a comfort in the chaos, I'll never forget August Grant Forkhill for giving me all that he has.

"Hey," Justin says as I get into his vehicle. He pulls off quickly, not allowing me to buckle my seatbelt first. I reply, "Hi, thanks for taking me." He smiles over his shoulder, "It's no problem, I'm glad I can help. Momma Cathy loves it when you visit. Even if it is just for your hair appointments."

"Is she at the salon now?" I ask, watching as he makes a left and approaches a stop sign. "Of course she is, you know she practically lives there," He responds, and I agree, she been working that shop for so long, I kind of hate how she gets no rest from it, and as stubborn as she is I don't see her willingly passing it down to one of her kids or grandkids for that matter and enjoying an easy retirement. "It's nice that she has you though," I say as the car pulls forward. He sighs, "Yeah, I wish it wasn't just me though."

After a while we pull up to the hair salon, and it's pretty busy inside which I'm actually grateful for. I take a seat near two other girls who I believe are next for her chair. I smile at them, and they nod. The one sitting further from me is a younger child, like maybe her mom dropped her off to get her hair done and will be back to pick her up later.

The other might be in her teens, she's taking down the remainder of her braids while she waits. Cathy's finishing up a teenager's cornrows. He's busy staring at his phone as she works but responds when she asks him to tilt his head or to hold something. I feel a familiar pang in my chest. Having to come to terms with leaving this place all over again.

When Cathy finishes, his mother comes out of nowhere, walking up to the counter to pay and Justin helps her. Cathy approaches me. "Hazel, it's always a joy to see you! What can I do for you? Have you finished the tea? I can whip you up a new jar!" She says a mouthful as she reaches me, pulling me into a hug.

I respond with a laugh, "Hi, Cathy." As she pulls back, she doesn't release my arms, looking me up and down, a smile spreads on her face, "No, you don't need that anymore, you need a prenatal blend." A laugh bubbles in my throat, and I gag on it, "I'm sorry what?"

Does she still think I'm trying to get pregnant, oh goodness. I shake my head, speaking kindly, "No, I'm here to get my hair redone Cathy, no more herbs." She looks at my hair and picks a few strands, "Okay we'll worry about that later, come and sit." I shake my head again because of the two girls that were here before me.

I point to them saying, "They were here first, I don't want to be rude." She waves them off and grabs my arm, "Nonsense child, they come here almost every week, they will be fine." I sit in her chair reluctantly, as she preps her supplies.

Once her magic fingers get to work, the guilt vanishes as I fall into the comfort of her presence. She removes the lace and washes the build up from it. Then, she washes my hair and redo's my braids, before reapplying the lace. Finally, she refreshes the curls, and I feel dainty and anew by the time I stand from her chair.

"Thank you," I say, feeling the blood rush back into my legs. She hugs me goodbye, "Don't worry about paying dear, It's always a pleasure." I smile, knowing I'll leave the cash with Justin because I'm just like everyone else, there's no reason for me not to pay, plus it feels good having my own money to do so.

She calls the younger girl to her chair, and I head to the front where Justin is. He perks up when he sees me, "Ready to go?" I nod paying first before we leave, "Yes, just one more stop." He tells Cathy he'll be back soon as he holds the door open for me.

I give Justin the address of the closest psych ward to town, hoping it's the correct one since I didn't pry for more information when August told me what happened to my mother. I still don't know how to feel about it, would her personality have changed if my dad never cheated? Would my dad have cheated if their relationship was better? I know these are questions I'll never get answers to and I'm not even sure why I want to see her before I go.

Justin doesn't ask many questions during the drive, and we arrive two towns over at the psych ward while the sun is still out. Going inside feels eerie, especially since I asked Justin to wait in the car, but I just want to say goodbye.

White walls and bright hospital lights greet me as I make it to the front desk. The waiting area is small, in fact this whole building looks small. A few black chairs line the waiting room walls; two dull landscape pictures hang near the desk.

There's only one or two other people here waiting, neither of them talking. "How can I help you?" The receptionist, dressed in white asks. I tell her I'm here to meet with my mother, Carla, and she asks a few more questions before handing me some paperwork to fill out.

After what feels like forever, I'm guided into a visiting room, where my mother is sitting impatiently. She looks so out of her element; Her natural hair is out in a bun, no makeup or jewelry. I see a white bracelet on her wrist, and she's dressed in plain white clothing.

It's like a curtain has been pulled back showing, under all her expensive clothes and dashing smile, she's just like the rest of us. When she finally sees me, disappointment then anger flash over her features. As I sit across from her, she fixes her face into a smile.

She begins, "Hazel sweetie, it's so good to see you!" Her voice full of warmth, she continues, "Have you had your fill of this little game? You ready to let me out of here now that you've shown me who's boss?" Even with the kindness in her tone, I can feel the venom seeping from her words. I reply, "I came to say goodbye."

Her face falls flat at my response, "We get it Hazel, you're big and bad now. You've got Mr. August Forkhill himself and now you think your shit don't stink." I'm surprised by her for a moment, she hasn't cursed since being married to my father. Always keeping her words and tone polished for anyone who might interest her, anyone to impress.

But there's no one else to impress anymore. "August isn't like you, mother, He-" I begin but she cuts me off. She exaggerates, "No of course not, he gets your little coochie wet, and suddenly he's your saving grace. You know, what *did* you come here for? I don't recall asking for you."

She turns her head to the side as if she's bored now, looking at her unmanicured nails as if they interest her. I open my mouth to respond, but the words don't come out. What did I come here for? To say goodbye, to let her know I was leaving? Like she'd care or worry if I stopped showing up for her. "You know what you're right," I begin.

"Always am," She responds under her breath without missing a beat. "Goodbye mother," I say standing and making my way to the door. As soon as I reach it she says, "Wait! Hazel darling, don't go. I'm just joking, this place is getting to my head." Warmth is present in her voice all over again and I shake my head. She still thinks she can control me, a puppet on strings to move at her will. Not anymore.

"Goodbye Carla," I say again walking out of the door. I can't move fast enough as I push back to the lobby.

"Hazel?"

I hear my name, which stops me in my tracks and look over my shoulder to see Thomas at the counter. Shit. I respond, cautiously, "Hi, Thomas. What are you doing here?"

"I'm dropping off these papers, I haven't seen you since the wedding, are you okay?" I try to smile wondering if I look bewildered, "Oh, I'm good, yeah." I nod to the papers in his hand, "Is that release papers?" He holds it up slightly, "These? No, divorce papers actually." I frown, "You're going to divorce her for being unstable?"

He shakes his head, "No, I'm divorcing her for infidelity. When your mother told me your dad was coming down to visit you, I thought great because I know how badly you wanted him at your wedding. I didn't think anything of it when your mom insisted on helping him while he was here, and imagine my surprise a few days after, when Jaxton shows up and my door and tells me how deep he was-" He stops himself, not finishing his sentence.

The look on my face must show how badly I do not want that image in my brain. Dammit too late, gross. He continues, "Anyway, I told her I love her no matter how difficult she is, but my one rule was loyalty, and she broke that."

Well, there goes husband number three, and she told him my dad was visiting me. Of course, she wouldn't tell him she called me a whore and convinced my dad I was whoring myself out and she *slept* with him. Wow we've come full circle. Whatever, she is not my problem anymore, "I'm sorry she did that to you."

He sighs, "Yeah well I better go deliver these papers." He pats my back as he leaves, and I feel a sense of weight fall from me. She's no longer my problem, not anyone's anymore.

The sun is setting as I find myself back in Justin's car he asks again, "Now you ready?" and I nod smiling. He takes me to the airport and insists waiting with me, "Are you sure?" We're standing at the curb; he's leaning against the passenger door of his car and I'm standing in front of him with my carry-on bag. "Yes, I am sure I'll be fine." No, I won't, I'm freaking terrified. A new place all by myself, and I can't even say goodbye to August.

"Okay, I just don't want this to be the last time I see you." He says, lifting off the side of the door.

I don't respond because truthfully, I don't know if it will be. He waves, opening the driver side door, "Until next time, Hazel Grace."

"It's Forkhill," I correct him, absentmindedly. Fuck why'd I just do that.

He only smiles at me as he gets in his car and drives off. I take a deep breath, and it's only now that the weight of my decision is crushing me. I haven't heard from August all day, and I can't call him or hug him goodbye, which I'd really, really love to do right now.

I walk into the small airport and take a seat ready to board when it's time. I'm supposed to be happy, but I feel the complete opposite. This is what I worked to achieve, so where are the butterflies? Why does my chest hurt with anxiety, and dread cloud my brain?

I take a deep breath again and pull my phone noticing I have a text message from August, sent five minutes ago. I open it quickly and it reads; *No matter how high you fly, I will be waiting for you. You will always be my Little Bird.*

My eyes begin to water and the ache in my chest intensifies, my heart feels heavy like stone, and my stomach twists in knots. I can't do this, this feels wrong. Just as I wipe the tears building in my eyes, the flight number for my plane is called and I can't bring myself to move my legs. The flight is called again, and still, I can't move. So, I call August.

His phone rings once, twice, a third time, and then he answers, "Hello?" I smile at his voice, it sounds uneven but it's him all the same, "Hi, August."

"Hi Little Bird," he says with emotion that pulls at my heartstrings. I take another deep breath, "So, what are you doing? I haven't heard from you all day." I try to sound casual as he clears his voice, "Funny story, I got a tattoo today."

"You got a tattoo?" I question in surprise as my eyes threaten to leak again. He laughs a little, "I did." I look around feeling out of place, "Well I'd love to see it."

I can hear his smile though he sounds sad as he says, "Do you want me to send you a picture?" I shake my head, "No, August, I want to see it in person." I take a deep breath and as I do the thoughts in my mind seal my fate, "I want to come home and see your tattoo in person."

After I told him where I was, August made it to the airport in no time. The night sky is covered in stars as I wait at the curb. He pulls up in front of me, throwing on the hazard lights, getting out of the car and asking, "Do you want to drive?" My face lights in excitement, "Yes!" He smiles, taking my bag, as we hurry into the car.

I silently thank him for letting me drive as it's a distraction from how I'm going to explain myself. I'm sure he didn't expect to see some of my things missing and a phone call from the airport. Still, he doesn't bring it the entire way home. He just rests his hand on my thigh as I drive and tells me the right directions when I forget.

As I pull into the driveway, I'm overwhelmed with the comfort of being back home. He carries my bag inside, letting me walk through the door first, and I turn on the living room light. "So," I begin unsure where to start. "You came back." He responds, shutting the front door behind him.

I turn to face him and now in the light I can fully drink him in. His hair is a mess on top of his head, His eyes look tired and red. He's dressed in a heather grey long-sleeved sweater and black sweats. All of him is covered, so I can't tell where that tattoo is, but he looks like a handsome mess. My handsome mess. I respond suddenly out of breath, "I did."

My brows knit momentarily, wait, did he know I was planning to leave? "You knew I was leaving?" I ask, standing in the middle of our living room. He responds using my exact words, "I did." Somehow, his answer hurts my feelings.

He knew I was leaving and didn't try to stop me? He didn't try to convince me to stay, would he have been fine with me gone? "You didn't…" I begin looking away from him as I pause to hide the pain in my voice.

He moves towards me, using his right hand to lift my chin, forcing me to look at him, "Hazel, I couldn't." He pauses, taking a deep breath, looks into my eyes and continues, "If you want to leave, I have no right to stop you. No matter how good being married to you is, I would never force you to stay if you are unhappy. I love you, Hazel. That means I'd give everything to see you happy, so if your happiness is somewhere else in the world. I wouldn't dare stand in your way."

His words seep into my soul and my eyes begin to water; dammit I don't want to cry. He said it, he said he loves me and my heart flutters in my chest. I wrap my arms around his neck, feeling his wrap around my waist. I can hear the subtle sound of plastic as my chest presses into his, "I love you too August and I am happy with you. I do want to travel and see more of the world, but I don't want to do it without you. You make me happy; you are my home. I want to spend every moment of every day with you."

My words seem to brighten the world around me as I can see our future together. He's it for me; I don't want what the world has to offer, without him beside me.

His arms tighten around me as his eyes show the same joy. I feel a buzz of happiness through my body, as he says, "Your forever mine then, Little Bird?" He poses it as a question, so I answer wholeheartedly, "I'm forever yours." As soon as my words leave my lips, he smiles crashing his lips into mine.

Held in his embrace, our kiss grows with passion and desperation. Heat spreads down my spine and blooms in my core. He is mine and right now, I want him. Pulling back, I fall to my knees, eager and pleased to see his cock hard and waiting for me. He grins down at me, "I thought you wanted to see my tattoo."

I quickly pull down his sweats and grab the base of his cock, licking my lips, I respond, "I do but I want your cock first." Feeling his cock throb in my hand, I immediately wrap my lips around him. He groans and the taste of him sets off my tastebuds. I hum around him keeping my eyes open as I take him further in my mouth then setting a pace. I want to see what I do to him.

"Fuck," He breathes out watching my every move. He lets me guide for a minute or so before he's gripping the back of my head and fucking my mouth. He moans and my pussy responds to his voice, making me desperate for him.He groans, pushing himself to the back of my throat before he pulls out. I gasp as he pushes me on to my back on the floor of our living room. He moves on top of me, removing my clothes like a ravenous man. "August," I whisper, he pulls my shirt over my head exposing breasts. "Mine," he finally says right before pulling down my bra and taking my nipple in his mouth. I gasp at the contact then hiss as he bites it. He lifts up hovering over me, "You're all mine Little Bird."

"Yes," I respond breathlessly, and he kisses my other boob before trailing kisses down my stomach and pulling down my pants as he goes. Fuck this is taking too long I just want his cock. I want to feel that familiar fullness of him inside me, claiming me, devouring me whole. "August, please," I beg.

His nose now rests above my pussy, and he inhales deeply before diving in. I gasp as pleasure runs through me, his tongue knowing the secrets of my body. Flicking and licking through every pathway to my soul.

I moan feeling an orgasm making itself known all too quickly. "Fuck August baby *please.*" I beg again. I need his cock; I need it like it's my last breath, but he doesn't stop. He continues his feast until I come on his tongue, and even then, he doesn't stop. The pleasure becomes unbearable as my clit feels numb. "August, wait it's too much!"

Finally, his head rises but only to respond, "I know you can come again, baby. Come for me one more time, and then I'll reward you with my cock." He doesn't wait for a response and when his tongue connects with my pussy, I cry out.

My back arches, and my hands find his head to try and push him away, but he's got a secure hold on my thighs "Fuck," I whisper the pleasure lights up all over my body. I have no choice but to get through it, and sure enough another orgasm creeps up on me like a storm. Washing over me violently, surging from my head to my toes, I moan through the wave focusing on breathing. My limbs feel weak as I come down, and August finally comes up.

He's smiling like a mad man, moving to lean over me, "Such a good girl aren't you baby?" He presses the head of his cock against my lips, rubbing against them, and I respond eagerly, "Yes!"

"Tell me your mine, Little Bird. Gift me your soul." He says pushing his head past my lips. He's teasing me, torturing me, pushing me into the blissful promised land of oblivion. "I'm yours baby, all yours, please I need to feel you inside me," I say breathlessly. I swear I'm on the brink of tears when I finally feel him sink into me.

"All mine," He responds, and a moan of relief leaves my lips as he watches me. He pulls out before sliding back in and setting a relentless pace. Groaning in his own pleasures, I bathe in the sound, getting lost in his voice and his cock.

In minutes he has me falling off the edge again, and he follows right behind me, leaving himself ball deep as I feel the hot ropes of his cum coating my walls.

Before we can catch our breaths, I say the words I feel in my soul, "I love you, August." He smiles down at me as he rests his weight on top of me, "I love you too Hazel baby, more then you'll ever know." He leans down to kiss me passionately.

Content, I pull back giggling, "Now, can I see your tattoo?" He rolls his eyes playfully, "I thought you'd never ask?" He finally pulls out of me as he sits up and as soon as he does, I feel his cum leaking out of me. He smiles at the sight before taking his shirt off and it dawns on me, he fucked me fully clothed. I don't know why but the thought turns me on again.

"Hazel baby," He calls me, pulling me back into the moment. I look at his face before my eyes land on his chest. Directly over his heart is a fresh tattoo of a black bird. It's a simple design, a filled in black bird with its wings outstretched and soaring, it's no bigger than the inside of my palm.

It dawns on me, it's me; his little black bird. He got it tattooed before I called him, when he still thought I was leaving. He tattooed a piece of me on him, knowing it'd be there forever, even if I wasn't. My heart swells and I lean up to kiss him saying, "Forever yours." He wraps his arms around me, kissing me back, "As I am yours, my love."

21. Epilogue

6 months later

The heat from the May sun beams on my skin. The sound of waves and crunching sand fill my ears as I lay on the beach waiting for August to return.

"One pistachio and one mango ice cream cone at your service," I hear his voice before I see him, opening my eyes as I struggle to sit up. "Thank you, my love," I respond as he squats on our beach blanket, sitting down beside me. I take both cones from his hands tasting one, then the other, and finally both together. The different flavors collide at first, melting into one and satisfying my taste buds.

"Well," August asks, waiting patiently, "Does our little guy like it then?" Licking my lips I respond, "He does." He smiles in return and we both look down at my growing belly.

Okay so maybe Cathy knows a little voodoo or something because she was right, I was pregnant that day I went to say goodbye, though I was in the early stages not even a month or so along. It could have been any one of the days we've had sex that I got pregnant, but I'd like to think it was the night I chose to stay, that night he made love to me like our souls depended on it. August thinks it was the night before, when he found out I was leaving and woke me out of my sleep for passionate lovemaking.

However, August and I didn't find out until we were two months into our honeymoon. I had to beg him not to cancel our trip. The plan was to travel for a whole year before returning to Springville, but I settled with the first six months of our pregnancy, determined to see the world before our baby boy arrives.

Which brings us to today, the last day of our honeymoon before we head back to our little hometown. Smiling, August reaches to rub my baby bump and we see little flutters of my skin as I feel him kick near August's hand. I smile, "I swear he always knows it's you, when you touch my stomach."

August laughs, moving down to kiss my stomach before swiping the pistachio ice cream from me and having a taste. His face immediately frowns, "That's disgusting I can't see how you think that tastes good." He shakes his head, handing it back and reaching for a water bottle. I laugh at him, "Blame your son." After he takes a sip he says, "Remind me again in three months."

There are only a few other people on the beach, but we're spread out enough, it almost feels like we're alone. I finish both icecreams, and August takes a nap beside me. As I watch the waves, I reminisce on our wedding day and how uneasy I was about marrying him. If I had to thank Carla for one thing, it would be for the arranged marriage with the son of a pastor.

"Welcome home!"

My heart rate spikes briefly before I recognize all the faces standing in our living room. "Hey guys," I laugh as August, and I enter our long-lost home. Lisa runs up to me first greeting my belly before pulling into a hug. I'm a little surprised, since August and I have been on the road, we've been the only people to touch my belly, I forgot people are handsy when it comes to pregnant people.

I hear John and Larson greet August beside me, all of their voices colliding into one loud noise. "It's so good to have you home!" Lisa beams, pulling away to hug August as Larson and John turn to greet me.

Finally, they step aside as Rachel waddles up to me, her stomach much larger than mine, as her due date is just around the corner. After her initial instruction on bedrest, she was approved to leave the house after reaching her third trimester and she's glowing. I know our friendship will never be close but it's really nice to have a sister I can chat with, and even more so now that we're both expecting.

We side hug as our stomachs are in the way and she asks, "It's nice seeing you again, Hazel. You look so beautiful." I thank her saying, "So do you. It's nice seeing you on your feet. I can't wait to see what your little girl looks like." Everyone moves further into the living room as Rachel and I sit down on the couch.

Lisa goes to grab a few glasses of water from the kitchen. Rachel rubs the underside of her belly responding, "Her name is Nevaeh, it's heaven spelled backwards. What about you guys? Have you named him yet?"

I playfully roll my eyes glancing at August who's still standing talking to Larson and John, "I want to name him Everson, but August wants his name to be June, a calendar baby like him." I laugh at the end of my sentence. I'm not totally against it though.

After another hour or so, everyone says their goodbye, leaving August and I, our privacy. As I close the front door, August walks up behind me, pressing himself into me, "Tell me who you belong to?" He pulls the collar around my neck. Really, it's just a gold necklace that I can't take off, literally, there's no clip. It pulls slightly against my throat.

I swear that man gets hard from hearing me say I belong to him. Instead, I tease him, "Hmm, I don't remember actually." I feel his cock hardening against me, his breath just above my right ear, "Oh really? That's a shame, I was looking forward to making you come, but it seems you'd much rather have a punishment instead?"

"Can't I have both?" I whine, still pressed against the door as arousal snakes through me. I feel his hand hook on the inside of my yoga pants before tugging them down, "We'll see." His hands rub over my ass before he pulls back and snacks it. The contact makes me jolt, I let out a small gasp and my pussy pulses. He grins saying, "You're mine Little Bird, Now let me hear you say it."

22. Extended Epilogue

AUGUST

Four years later

The dimming light from the sunset beams through our bedroom window, allowing me to see the stretch marks that litter Hazel's skin as I watch from beside her as she lays naked in bed.

The evidence of time and our love paint her curves, it amazes me how I got to watch her body change during the growth of our son, June Everson Forkhill, then feeling helpless as I watched her battle the valley of death to bring him into the world. I don't think there was a moment in time before that I've ever been so proud of my wife.

"What are you staring at?" She looks over her shoulder at me confused. I smile at her, "You of course." She rolls her eyes, "Have you checked the time? How much longer do I have to wait like this?" I smirk at her, quickly checking my watch, "You've got two more minutes." She rolls her eyes again, smacking her lips, "I don't remember it being this hard the first time."

It's true, though we weren't purposely trying back then, getting pregnant seemed to happen a lot faster. The second time around feels like it's taking more effort. I respond, "Well the first time, we didn't have a raging four-year-old that needs our daily attention." She laughs, "Do you think he's missing us right now?" I shake my head, "June's at his grandparent's house; he probably hasn't thought about us since we dropped him off this morning." Hazel laughs in agreement.

Finally, the timer goes off and I stand, moving to the end of the bed, already dressed for the evening. Today's our monthly *adults only* hangout with Daniel, Caleb and my brother. My two best friends I'm entirely grateful for, even more so now that we have June, it's nice to escape parenthood sometimes.

"Thank goodness." Hazel says as she sits up, and I see my cum slide down her leg and my cock pulses as if I didn't just rail her for the past hour. I groan trying to will the blood rush elsewhere, saying, "We'll try again later, for good measure." She smirks at me as I watch her get dressed and when she's done the front door rings. Perfect timing.

We leave our bedroom, passing by my old office that we turned into June's bedroom and make our way to the front door. Hazel opens the door revealing Rachel and Larson she beams, "Hey guys, come on in!" Rachel and Larson both look tired, yet excited to be here, I laugh to myself, I'm sure that's thanks to their girls, Nevaeh, and Emily.

"I brought beer!" Larson says grinning as he holds up a twelve pack. They shuffle in and we make our way to the kitchen. "We'll get the fire started," I say as Larson follows me to the back yard. Hazel and Rachel nod before giggling about something in the kitchen. I'm glad Hazel has Rachel; she swears she can't stand her sometimes, but I think their first pregnancy made them closer.

"You have no idea how much I look forward to these nights, brother," Larson tells me, patting me on the back. I flip on the porch light as I close the sliding door behind us, and we move to the fire pit in the center of my backyard. "You and me both," I say in agreement. I've already set us a few chairs around the pit and Larson plops down in one, immediately opening a can of beer and handing me one.

I grab it, nodding my thanks as he watches me grab a few logs and arrange them in the fire pit. "You know I never thought I'd see the day," He begins. I take a sip of my beer and question him, "What do you mean?"

He does the same before spreading his arms out around him, "All of this. Dad retiring and me taking over the church full-time. Rachel quitting that café job and now teaching our youth. I never thought I'd have everything I wanted, my girls, my wife, and the church. God is good, man. God is good."

I snicker taking another sip, "Don't go getting all preachy on me, save that shit for the church." He laughs at my response but doesn't respond as I move to finally light the pit. Soon enough the flames are flickering, lighting up Larson's face and the surrounding chairs.

I move to sit in a chair as I hear the sliding door open. Out comes Hazel and Rachel with chips, dip, and a charcuterie board. Hazel leans down to kiss me before sitting down beside me with the dip and chips in her lap.

Where the Hell are Daniel and Caleb? I pull out my phone, sending a message in our group chat, saying; *you fuckers on your way?*

Almost immediately Daniel responds, saying they're almost here. Caleb responds the same, telling me not to get my boxers in a twist. I scoff, laughing to myself and putting my phone away.

I look at everyone around me, engaging in small talk and relaxing a little. Larson is right, I've never felt so fucking lucky.

Sneak Peak of The Son of a Ghost Book 2 in the Springville Trilogy

Chapter One

Elizabeth

Present

I hate the heat, and I hate driving.

God must hate me because I'm driving in the middle of May's heat to this town called Springville. At least I would be if my car's check engine light didn't come on and now has me stuck roadside.

My eyes are tired from crying, and a lump still feels stuck in my throat. It's dark out and there's no summer breeze, just thick stale heat.

I sigh, seeing the town sign right before picking up to call my mother but decide against it. I made it here, right? No need to worry her right now, so instead I quickly look up and call the local mechanic shop.

Someone answers in two rings his voice raspy, as if just awaking, "McCarter's Mechanics. How can I help you?" It's an older man's voice on the line. "Hi, my car's broken. I mean my car broke down and it's the middle of the night, any chance you can send someone to help me?"

He laughs and the sound of a bed creaking plays in the background, "Don't worry darling, I'll send to the tow on over and have them bring you to the shop? Can you tell me your general location?"

I sign in relief, "Yeah, I think I'm just at the town line. Near the Springville welcome sign." I look around to see anymore landmarks, "There's also what looks like an abandoned church nearby."

"Okay, I know just where you are, hold on tight!" He hangs up the phone without asking for my name or a call back number. Tears threaten my eyes as if my day couldn't get any worse.

I grab my keys praying this is all a fluke and turn the ignition, "Come on Betsy." She makes the worse skidding sound and I stop. "Dammit!" I yell looking at myself in the mirror.

The darkest shade of brown fills my iris and red stains my outer eyes from all the tears. Freckles cover my brown skin as my thick thighs fill the seat, sitting on top of my head are my fresh twenty-eight-inch boho braids. "At least my hair is done," I whisper as the sound of the night's creepy crawlers fill the air. The darkness makes the nearby trees feel eerily haunting.

I'm not sure how much time passes when big bright lights spot me from head on, thank God. I check my yellow bodycon sundress to make sure there's no stains and grab my phone as I move to stand outside of my car.

I begin to wave the closer it gets, as if I'm not the only car stuck out here in the middle of a quiet town. I can see the silhouette of the driver as the truck slows and passes my car to do a U-turn before pulling in front of my vehicle.

Avery tall man comes into view, it's too dark to see his features, but his hair looks short, almost moplike, and his voice rings like velvet in the air, "You mind if I take a look under the hood before hooking it up? It might be an easy fix, like a loose wire." I nod, "Yeah no problem." I go to pop the hood as he moves to grab a flashlight before moving to the front of the car.

I watch as he bends with the flashlight to look under the hood. My phone pings with a back to back text message that I ignore. "Aren't you going to see who texted you?" he asks, not taking his eyes off of my car's intestines. "Nope," I reply popping the p. I already know who it is, and after what I just saw, He doesn't deserve another lick of my time.

I sigh, *my time*, so much wasted. "What's your name?" I ask him to distract myself. "The names Daniel, Daniel McCarter." I nod. "Nice to meet you, I wish it was under different circumstances," I laugh a little pointing to my Betsy.

"No worries, it's a pleasure meeting you too," He responds standing up to his full height. I gulp, is he really that tall or am I just short, well I mean I know I'm short so he's probably not that tall, right?

He approaches me asking, "When's the last time you had your car serviced?" Nope he's really freaking tall, 6ftmaybe. His figure nearly crowds mine. I shrug my shoulders, "Last year, maybe."

He shakes his head laughing in response, "Figures, it looks like the wires on your batteries have burnt to a crisp. I'm not sure how long you were driving but it looks like it fried along the way. Let's take it back to the shop and I'll see if we have a replacement."

"Okay," I agree, thankful it's not a major fix. I wait as I watch him hook up my Betsy to his tow truck before he asks, "What's your name?" I frown in confusion, I thought we went over introductions already, "What?"

"Well, I told you mine, so don't I get the pleasure of knowing yours," He smiles as he follows me to the passenger side of the cab. "My name's Elizabeth, but people call me Liz," I say as he holds cab door open for me. If I wasn't so upset from all the events of today, I'd appreciate the gesture. I wait as he closes it behind me and heads over to the driver's side.

Once inside he asks, "So what brings you to Springville?"

"Family," I say lying, well partially. "Are you moving to town?" he says. I sigh shaking my head, "I haven't though that far ahead." I just wanted to drive, and my mind brought me here. He says,

"Ah, so just going with the flow then." I reply, "At the moment that's what it seems."

I look at his hands on the steering wheel, which are bare of any rings. He's about to ask something again but beat him to it, "You like to talk, don't you?" He smiles and the growing irritation inside me withers away.

His smile is bright and inviting, it sends warmth floating in the small cab around us. I sigh, I should be nice, after everything I've just been through, I could use a friend.

**Book 2 Release Date Coming Soon!
Keep a look out on my Instagram
@booksbyamber118 or my website ww
w.amrbooks.com**

Acknowledgments

I can't believe I've made it to my second book seeing the light of day. I want to thank you, the reader. With your support my dream of being an author is coming true. I want to thank my sister for being my hype man and my love for being my everything and more.

Thank you to my beta readers, who saw this story in its rawest and most distressed form and still had hope. To my arc readers for hyping my head up lol, and to my promo babes for their support on and off social media.

I owe it to you all, thank you.

About the Author

Amber Rodriguez is a spicy romance author who lives in a small town in California. She's a likes hot coffee, slow mornings, and all things nature and cottage core inspired. Spicy romance books have her heart, and she writes poetry on the side.

If you'd like to connect with her, you can find her on;

Website: www.amrbooks.com

On Instagram @booksbyamber118

On TikTok @booksbyamber118

On Facebook @Author Amber Rodriguez

Did you enjoy The Son of a Pastor? Check out other works by Amber Rodriguez

<u>StandAlone</u>
Beautiful Chaos
<u>Springville Trilogy</u>
The Son of a Pastor
The Son of a Ghost
Book 3

BOOK ONE IN THE SPRINGVILLE TRILOGY

THE SON OF A PASTOR

AMBER RODRIGUEZ